FIGHT
Back

FIGHT Back

MOTHER'S CAN BE BULLIED TOO

DR. MELVIN J. BAGLEY

TATE PUBLISHING
AND ENTERPRISES, LLC

Published by Tate Publishing & Enterprises, LLC
127 E. Trade Center Terrace | Mustang, Oklahoma 73064 USA
1.888.361.9473 | www.tatepublishing.com

Tate Publishing is committed to excellence in the publishing industry. The company reflects the philosophy established by the founders, based on Psalm 68:11,
"The Lord gave the word and great was the company of those who published it."

Book design copyright © 2014 by Tate Publishing, LLC. All rights reserved.
Cover design by Ivan Charlem Igot
Interior design by Mary Jean Archival

Published in the United States of America

ISBN: 978-1-63367-126-3
1. Fiction / Family Life
2. Family & Relationships / Bullying
14.10.23

To all my beautiful grandchildren: Parris, Jessica, Andrew, Athena, Hannah, Jeri, Theodore, Calli, Aris, Jaylin, and Gabriel

1

Amy felt a familiar knot form in the pit of her stomach as she opened the third collections letter she had received that month. It was reminding her that if she did not pay a minimum balance soon, she'd be turned into collections. She scanned the letter but didn't need to; she knew what it said. She'd seen so many of the same kinds of letters, she could write them herself. When she got to the end, she walked into her home office and put the letter with the others. This was not what she imagined life to be at forty-two years old.

Amy Glade had big dreams when she was a kid. She grew up in a suburb outside of Oklahoma City where she studied hard and went on to what she believed was the best university in the state, the University of Oklahoma. There she studied

German, literature, and creative writing for four years. It was her aspiration to write a book that someone else would study at a university one day. At twenty-one, she believed it was possible; at that time she believed that nothing was out of her reach. Somehow, that had changed drastically over the years.

Her junior year of college, Amy met a young man named Dale Glade; he was getting a masters in finance and had already mastered the art of being a lady killer. Dale had been in a fraternity throughout his undergrad, and he made sure to live the clichéd life of a frat boy. Dale drank, hazed, and slept around with the best of them. Where Amy spent all her extra time in the library, Dale spent his at social events, plotting out who in the room he could sleep with or who might benefit him as a connection in the long run. That was his idea of taking control of his future. "It's not what you know, it's who you know" was an axiom the young socialite lived by. It had served him and his family well too.

Dale had been raised in a fairly small town about an hour away from Oklahoma City, where he was molded in the "big fish in a small pond" syndrome. His family had money from the mineral rights off of land his great granddad bought long before Dale was ever even thought of. The land and the money stayed in Dale's family, and so his last name carried him quite a ways in his little community. It carried him so far, in fact, that Dale could do about anything he wanted around town without consequences. Along with the notoriety he had from his family, he had also been an all-star athlete in his

Class 2A school, but his ego was large enough for the pros. He was first string quarterback and a championship wrestler, the latter of which he continued on with in college. He brought his big-fish attitude to the college town of Norman, Oklahoma, and somehow made it work there too.

By the time Amy met Dale, he had outgrown his fraternity days to some degree, and he had also decided he was ready to settle down, to some degree. It was around that time that a friend of his introduced Amy to him. She was petite, with long auburn hair, and eyes that had a way of making a person's stomach flutter when she looked into theirs; they flashed and showed that something intense was hiding beneath her meek exterior. She was extremely intelligent and nothing like the countless girls Dale had coaxed into his bed. In the beginning, he was drawn to the way Amy didn't mess around like the other girls he knew. He was still distracted by those girls, but he knew Amy was the kind of girl a guy settled down with, and so he pursued her. Dale was a good-looking guy himself, standing at a little over six feet tall and having maintained his athletic build from wrestling four years in college. He also knew how to impress others, and so he won Amy over with his charm. Two years after their first date, the two married. And that is when Amy began to see that charm can only carry someone so far. She also began to see that he had not completely grown out of his fraternity days.

Dale ultimately left graduate school; he decided that he'd made enough connections to get him to where he was headed.

He was offered a job as a teller at a bank in a quaint little town about forty-five minutes outside of Oklahoma City, where a former frat buddy of his named Collin Drake worked. Collin promised quick upward mobility, and Dale liked the idea of being back in a smaller town, and so he jumped at the opportunity. That was right around the time the two were married, so Dale's father wrote the newlyweds a check for a sizable down payment on their first home, which was on Main Street in the town of Hennessey, Oklahoma, where Dale assumed he would be shooting up the latter at work in no time and be able to take on the monthly mortgage, which was just slightly outside their means. Unfortunately, Collin misrepresented the job and the opportunities, and Dale saw no upward movement in his new career. He also had some archaic values that stunted the couple.

Something Amy had noticed throughout their engagement was the way Dale viewed his mother. Dale's mother had never worked in her life, and according to him, "that was the way God intended it." Amy was a little unsettled by his fleeting comments but tried to brush them off. After their marriage, however, she learned a hard lesson in paying attention to red flags.

"So I guess you'll go ahead and quit your job then," Dale said just before their wedding day.

Amy had been doing freelance writing for local magazines and was also a copy editor for a little publication that circulated around the college town. She loved both jobs dearly and hoped they would lead to her dream of publishing her own book one day.

"Why would I quit my job?" she asked, confused.

"Because being my wife will be your job," he told her matter-of-factly.

"I can't be your wife and have a career?"

"Pfph!" he scoffed. "I think I have made that pretty clear, Amy."

"But I love my…"

"Amy, we're going to have kids someday. That is what you will do—raise them. My job is to provide, and yours is to raise our family," he said firmly, leaving no room for debate.

"I can do both," she replied softly.

"I said I'm going to take care of you, just like my dad did our family," he insisted.

"But I want to…"

"That's enough, Amy. I love you, and I'm going to be the breadwinner. Period. That's how I was raised, and that's how it'll be. It's only natural."

The conversation left Amy unnerved, but she thought that he'd let go of his antiquated notion of men and women by the time they actually got married. She assumed he'd appreciate the extra income as they got on their feet. She found out soon enough that she was wrong. As soon as they moved out to their new home in Hennessey, Dale put his foot down and ended Amy working at all, even though she could have done it from home. His entry-level pay, combined with her lost income, put them immediately in troubled waters as far as finances went. Where she should have been in the honeymoon phase, excited about her new life with Dale, Amy felt an unshakable sense of foreboding and wondered how they'd ever make it at the rate they were going.

"This is just for now," Dale repeated constantly to his wife as they struggled to make ends meet with his teller job. "I'm the best they got. It'll be me giving orders in no time. I'm telling you, I'll be the VP in no time. Hell, I'll be the president before five years is up."

"I can get a job to bring in extra money in the meantime," she suggested.

"You're my wife, Amy. My wife does not work," he told her, red-faced and resolute.

Amy looked down at her wedding band every time the two got into the discussion. She was born and raised Catholic, and so she knew that she had gotten herself into something now that she would have to make work, regardless of her husband's stubbornness. When an EPT came back positive just four months after the wedding, she felt that perhaps Dale was right all along; perhaps it was best she stayed home. It was either agree or be resentful anyway, and she did not believe she could resent her husband and keep a good standing with the Man upstairs. And so Amy threw herself into the role of mother and tried to love her lot as best she could. Instead of pushing to get a job, Amy resigned to her fate and did all she could to help her husband move ahead. She stayed active in the community to promote him, took on all the duties at home so he could work late and hobnob with his higher-ups, and she even suggested that he return to finish his masters so that he would have an edge on the competition, which he refused to do because he insisted he had everything under control. Nothing seemed to ever pan out for her husband at work though. With all she did to help him move ahead, Amy could not figure out why her husband's career was so stagnant.

"Why don't we invite Clark and Jason over for dinner?" she'd suggest. Clark and Jason were the president and vice president of the bank. "This way you can be home with the family instead of spending time out. I think it would personalize things for them, too, to sit down with me and Andrew."

"I don't think so," he'd say without giving her suggestion a shot.

"Why not?"

"Let me handle business and you handle the house, okay?"

Amy learned to stay quiet eventually and let her husband make the decisions. It seemed that her attempts to help only made him angry with her. She also found that he met her suggestions with insults, and she wanted to avoid his stinging remarks, especially once their son Andrew was old enough to comprehend what was going on. She had been raised in a house in which her father insisted on the family respecting their mother, and so she wanted the same to be instilled in her son. She knew that if she wanted to do that, she would just have to do all she could to avoid her husband's biting remarks because he was not going to hold his tongue.

2

Years passed, and Dale barely inched his way up at the bank; but for reasons Amy could not understand, he still insisted on staying there.

"Maybe if we moved to Oklahoma City," she suggested at one point, six years after they saw no signs of advancement. "You know, in these small banks no one ever retires. If you went to a large branch, there would be tons more opportunity for promotions and pay raises," she urged.

"We're staying right where we are," he told her.

"It's been six years, babe," she reminded him gently so as not to put him on the defense. Everything put Dale on the defense, however.

"I don't need you to remind me of how long I've worked somewhere, Amy," he spat.

"What do you think about me doing something to make some extra money now that Andrew is in school? I have the time now," she suggested.

"I'll not be the laughing stock of my family and this town because I couldn't do my job," he snorted. "I don't know why you don't get that, Amy."

"Women work all the time, Dale," his perturbed wife blurted, unable to keep her frustration at bay. "This isn't 1952!"

"This is *my* house, damnit!" he fumed. "*My* house, and I will say what goes on in it!"

"I just want to help," Amy started to cry.

"Help me by supporting me then instead of fighting with me," Dale roared. "I married you because I thought you'd make a good wife," he added coldly.

Those words stung Amy's spirit like lemon juice on a fresh cut. When he let them go, they seeped deep down into gashes that were already there because of what kind of disappointment Dale had been as a husband. Amy could hardly believe that he had the nerve to say what he had just said. It had been less than a year since Amy found out about one of Dale's many affairs. *She* had been the laughing stock of the town. *She* was the one who knew what it felt like to have people whispering as she walked by. And through all that, she had decided to stay with him. *He* had trampled on the vows they made and betrayed her like no one had, but she stayed, only to have him stand there and suggest that she was the one not fulfilling her duties as a wife. Every mistake Dale had made bubbled up to the surface of her consciousness: coming home drunk, the lies, his spending when they had nothing, the girls! Just as she was going to say something, she heard the door slam. It was Andrew coming in from playing outside with the neighborhood children.

"Mom?" he called out from the front room. She could hear his voice was trembling; he was upset.

"I'm here, sweetheart," she called back as she left Dale in the bedroom to check on their son.

"What's wrong, sweetheart?" she asked as she pulled her son to her.

"I just wanna stay in here with you, okay?" he cried. "I just don't wanna go back out."

"Did something happen?" she asked.

"Let him be," Dale bellowed down the hall. "He needs to be a man, not a sissy."

Amy's eyes narrowed as she whipped her head in Dale's direction. Her face softened and she turned back to her son, comforting him saying, "Pay him no mind, honey. What's going on?"

"I just wanna stay in and play," he said as he sniffed back his tears. "Is that okay?"

"Sure, sweet boy," Amy consoled her son.

Andrew was five at the time, and he didn't seem to have the arrogance his father did. In fact, it looked as though he was extremely tender-hearted, just like his mother. Amy had noticed his sensitive disposition from the time he was about one, and she had also noticed Dale's disapproval. Being an all-star athlete and a man's man, Dale cringed at his son's sensitivity. Both Amy and Andrew began to enjoy the nights Dale was out doing whatever it was he did. The house was calm and happy on those evenings.

Amy let the awful comment Dale slide and never brought it up again, but she didn't stop pushing for some kind of remedy to their financial problems. She may have made a vow to stay in her marriage until death did them part, but she also felt she had to fight for a better life for her son. He was only five, so he didn't feel the strain of being broke too much yet. She knew in time he would, however. She yearned to do what she could to save him from a life of need. As a mother, her heart was set on protecting her little boy. She was resolved to do just that.

One day while she was out running errands, Amy ran into a friend who had a son Andrew's age. Her name was Shelly, and Amy had met her through play dates with their sons. She knew that she was a stay-at-home mom as well, but could see she was in a business suit that day. Amy stopped to chat with her play-date acquaintance quickly.

"You look great!" she said as the two waved and walked toward one another in the parking lot of the local grocery store.

"Oh, thanks!" Shelly replied. "I'm off to show a house."

"I didn't know you worked."

"I got a license in real estate a few months back, and I just do a little here and there," Shelly told her. "It's a great little side project to take on for some extra money. All the activities for the boys get so expensive, you know! Sports and camps and who knows what else is coming!"

"Oh, I know," Amy agreed, and suddenly she realized that Shelly may just be a genius.

The two said their good-byes and Amy went home that night to present Dale with a new plan; she wanted to get a license in real estate. She was sure to phrase it just right and assure him it didn't mean she would go to work anytime soon. She worked hard to make it seem it was his idea, as that was the only way to get Dale to agree to anything.

"I saw Shelly Sanders today and she mentioned this real estate school she went to. It was just during the day for a few hours and now she can sell her own house."

"Hmm," Dale grunted, hardly listening.

"I just thought it sounded kind of interesting," Amy said. "It only takes a few months and I thought it'd give me something to do since Andrew is in school all day."

"So you want to sale real estate then?"

"Not really," she backpedaled, sensing his disapproval. "I just thought it'd be interesting and could come in handy if we ever wanted to look into it. With you being the vice president of the bank someday, I might learn something that'd be of interest in the classes. Plus it would keep me out of the stores during the day while Andy is at school," she added to sell her idea.

"If that's what you want to do," he said and turned the TV on. "But we don't have the money now."

"It is," she said. "And I've already realized if I just keep two kids during the day for a while, I could save up the money to pay for it. I'd still be home, but I could save up the money myself."

"I guess," he said after some thought. "Just make sure the house doesn't turn into a zoo."

Amy set out to find parents in Andrew's class that needed after-school care, and she kept two children for a year to save up enough to pay for her school in full. As soon as she had the money, she started classes. Within a few months, she had her license. While taking day classes, she learned a lot and was glad to be doing something that used her mind in a new way again. Unfortunately, any time she suggested using the license, Dale shot her down. After a year of rejection, Amy quit trying, until one day nearly ten years later when Dale came home with news that put them in a place he couldn't say no anymore.

"They let me go," Dale slurred as he sunk down into the sofa. He reeked of alcohol and it was only two in the afternoon.

"They what?" Amy asked in shock.

"I said they let me go!" he howled.

"Andrew is going to be home before long, Dale. He can't see you like this."

"Forget about that, Amy. We are gonna lose it all! You wanna tell him that when he turns sixteen there won't be any car?"

"Why did…what happened?"

"No business. Economy is shit, and so they're cuttin' people. And I was one they cut. How 'bout that? Sixteen years I've been there and not so much as a severance package. F——k them," he snarled.

"We'll figure something out," Amy insisted, trying to stay optimistic.

"I should burn the place to the ground," he mumbled.

Dale got up and disappeared into their bedroom. Amy was glad because Andrew was about to be home from school and she didn't want him to see his father in the belligerent state Dale was in. As she waited, she paced the kitchen and tried to think of a solution. All she could think about was her real estate license. She had kept it up-to-date even though she had never used it, but it looked to her like it was the perfect time to get Dale to agree to finally letting her try her hand at real estate. The next day when she suggested it, however, Dale was still avidly against it.

"What else will we do then?" Amy asked, desperate and frustrated. "It seems ridiculous not to try in the state we're in. Andrew is already the only kid who doesn't get to go on vacations or any summer camps. We can't cut anything else. We need money to live, Dale. I could help," she pleaded.

"I'm filing for unemployment today," he told her.

"Unemployment?" she asked a little confused.

"Yeah," he answered. "I don't have a choice."

"I could try real estate," she urged.

"We need money now, Amy. If that worked at all, it could be months."

"Couldn't you take a loan from your dad?"

"Like hell!" Dale shouted. "I'll sell my kidney before I do that."

"Dale, I just think that…"

"Amy," Dale said cutting her off, "I am the man of the house and I will take care of this. Okay? Why don't you ever just trust me? Why do you get the idea in your head that my job is something for you to worry about?"

Amy sat looking away without saying a word, so he repeated himself, "I am the man of the house."

"Okay," Amy acquiesced, holding back her tears.

Later that day, he went to the unemployment agency to fill out his paperwork so he would start receiving unemployment checks. He also started scouring the newspapers for jobs. Week after week, he saw nothing that he felt suited him. The jobs he did feel were up to his standards never called back for a second interview. When he finally came to terms with the fact that he was in desperate need of a job no matter what, the only job available in the area that wasn't construction or farmwork was as a fast-food restaurant manager. With no other choices and with bills piling up, he took the job. As much as working in fast food chipped away at his pride, he knew that his family needed money immediately. They had already been late on the mortgage so many times that the mortgage company had no more patience with them. They also had accumulated a sizable amount of credit card debt trying to tread water over the years.

"I'm going to work for Wilson's Burger Shack," he told Amy after his first job interview. While the bank didn't seem to take to Dale, the fast-food joint was beyond impressed with his credentials. When the hiring manager told Dale what the annual salary was, however, he knew that there was no way they could make it on his salary alone anymore, especially if they wanted to keep their home.

"How much will you make?" Amy asked reluctantly.

"Not enough," he answered.

"I am still willing to work," she told him. "I mean, Andrew is a teenager now and able to do most everything himself, so I…"

"Do it," he said finally. "We need whatever we can get.

Amy set out to find a real estate job, and with Shelly's help, she did in no time. The downside to her career choice was that the job was based on commission, which meant she saw no money until she made a sale. Amy was very personable and believed that even if it was commission-based, she would do well in the field. She was right too. In the first three weeks, she was able to make a small sale. They weren't going to be able to get Andrew a new car anytime soon, but the extra money did get all the bills paid and put food on the table. Still, though, they were scraping just to get by. With the economy on the downhill slide, everything was suffering, especially real estate. Amy was determined to find a solution, however.

3

While the Glades were scrounging to make ends meet, another family issue arose that was as concerning to Amy as their financial problems. Andrew was having trouble at school with a couple of bullies. Amy knew that her son was sensitive but had hoped he would be an athlete like his father, as she felt that perhaps being an athlete would ward off any foul-mouthed jerks. While Andrew did have his father's lean, muscular build, he did not become heir to his love for sports. He also inherited his mother's petite frame, which made him a bit of a target for fork-tongued boys looking to tear down whoever they could. Of course, when Andrew started coming home day after day complaining about the boys who were bullying him, Dale had no empathy; he had been the bully himself when he was in school.

"Quit giving them ammunition." He'd chuckle when Andrew mentioned the way the other boys treated him.

"They call me names for just walking by!" Andrew would blurt, upset that his father wouldn't take his side.

"Boys call people names, Andy. Be a man and deal with it."

"They shouldn't," Amy would interject. "Those kids are awful for tearing others down and they're wrong for it," she fumed.

"He needs to quit being such a cry baby. Maybe if he didn't come crying to his mommy, they'd ease up."

"Enough," Amy boomed. She rarely got loud with her husband, but he was crossing lines she would not stand for.

One night after Andrew had mentioned being bullied again, Amy went into his room to talk, just the two of them. She had seen far too many news stories of kids taking their own lives because of incessant bullying to simply brush Andrew's problems off as callously as her husband had.

"You want to tell me what's going on, kiddo?"

"It's stupid. Never mind," Andrew clammed up.

"It isn't, sweetie. It isn't at all, and I want to hear what's going on. I want you to know this is their problem, not yours. There is nothing wrong with you, it's them."

"If I weren't a sissy, they'd just leave me alone," Andrew said, his chin quivering.

"No, they wouldn't. Those boys don't like themselves, so they take it out on people who have hearts. Don't think for a second that makes it your fault."

"I must've done something to make them hate me."

"That is not true at all, Andy. Don't ever think that."

"Whatever, it's no big deal," Andrew withdrew.

"It is. And I want to know all that's going on, Andy."

"It's just some of the bigger jock guys being assholes."

"What are they doing? Do they ever threaten you?"

"No, not really. They just call me a lot of names that you probably don't want me to repeat. They basically say I'm a huge sissy, and they also say stuff about Dad and how we are poor."

"What about Dad?"

"Nothing."

"Hon, it's okay."

"It's just crap—stuff about how he will do..." Andrew stopped himself.

"It's okay, honey."

"I really don't wanna say, Mom. They just say he's a loser and I'm gonna be like him, except I'm a little twerp so I'll be even worse. They say stuff about how we're gonna be homeless because he can't get his stuff together and ask if you have to prostitute yourself out to keep our house and stupid crap like that."

"That's disgusting and untrue," Amy said with a shudder.

"I know, Mom. They're just idiots trying to get to me. Sometimes they rough me up some."

"They what?" Amy blurted.

"It's no big deal, Mom," Andrew insisted, regretting having said it.

"What do they do?"

'Don't go crazy here, Mom. If you do, it'll get worse for me. I'm not saying anything else if you are going to go nuts."

"I won't. I promise. I just want to know," she assured him.

"They shove me into lockers or spit wads at me during class. Sometimes they shove me around in the hall or mess with my food at lunch."

Amy could feel her blood burning hot on the surface of her skin. She felt tears well up at the edges of her eyes, but she willed them away so her son wouldn't see her pain. She took a deep breath and thought about what he said. The thought of going to the school and complaining to the principal crossed her mind, but she knew that would make things harder for Andrew. After a little time of thinking it over carefully, she settled on a different plan.

"You should stand up for yourself, sweetie," she finally said.

"What do you mean?"

"Fight back," she said, with her fists clenched into tiny white balls. "You should fight back."

"But I'd just get the crap beaten out of me," he said. "Or I'd get in trouble."

"Wait until you aren't on school property," she said, her words sounding like they came from someone else. Amy had always been a pacifist and never believed in eye for an eye retribution, but she suddenly saw that her son would never be left alone unless he stood his ground.

"They'll annihilate me though," he told her.

"Remember Dad's friend James? The one he wrestled with in college?" Amy said, remembering that Dale had an old college buddy who was a wrestling coach about thirty minutes away.

"Sort of. What about him?"

"He's a wrestling coach—a championship wrestling coach. If I remember right, he gives private lessons. You're going to start taking them as soon as I can get a hold of him."

"We can't afford that, Mom," Andrew said.

"You let me worry about that," she insisted. "I'll get the details worked out."

"Really?" Andrew asked hopefully.

"You bet, kiddo. You don't have to take that, and I'm going to make sure you won't anymore."

"That'll actually be kinda cool, I guess." Andrew smiled.

"Here's the thing though, Andrew," Amy said with a grave expression. "This is to protect yourself and that is all. It is not to become a bully. Nietzsche said, 'Be careful when fighting the monster, lest you become a monster yourself.' I want you to remember that."

"I have no idea who that is, Mom, but I promise not to become a monster."

"So wrestling practice it is. I'll let you know when we start." Amy smiled as she squeezed her son's leg. "And this is for defense only. The last thing you want is to be like those jerks. You're too good for that." She smiled and kissed Andrew's head.

Amy tracked James down, and he got Andrew in immediately. They started doing private lessons three days a week, on the days Dale was at work late. Amy paid for the lessons by cleaning a few houses that were on the market for her company. Just two weeks after he started his wrestling, three of the guys that had been harassing him found Andrew walking home from school and decided to remind him what a wimp he was. The biggest of the guys, an oaf named Jared who was known to knock guys and girls around if he didn't get his way, started name-calling, and so Andrew picked up his pace. Jared wasn't going to let him off so easy, so he grabbed Andrew by the neck of his jacket.

"I'm talking to you, little girl," Jared mocked as he pulled Andrew toward him.

Andrew spun out of the grip of the bulky antagonist and swept the kid's legs so that he went crashing to the sidewalk. Andrew twisted the felled giant into a pretzel and whispered into his ear, "I hope you're done with this, because I'm not putting up with your shit anymore."

"Just get off me!" Jared cried out, his arm throbbing where Andrew had it twisted behind his broad back.

"Are you gonna leave me alone?" he asked.

"Whatever, man, just get the hell off me," Jared murmured as his sidekicks backed away from the two boys who were tangled together on the ground.

"I mean it, no more," Andrew said as he straightened his clothes and walked away.

From that day forward, no one talked about Andrew or his family, nor did they shove him in halls or spit on his food at lunch. Andrew suddenly didn't feel like the smallest guy in school, either. He may have been only five feet and five inches tall, but he felt like he was just as big as anyone in his class. It was then that Amy got the idea for the book she had dreamed of writing since she was a college student at OU.

"You've inspired me, kiddo," she said to her son one evening over dinner.

"What do you mean?"

"I'm going to write a book."

"What about?"

"About you in a way. I'm going to call it *Fight Back*. I think it could be something that could help people everywhere. It would let people all over the country see that there is a better solution to bullying than a mother running down to the school to complain. It'll show that we have to give our kids the power to stand up." She smiled.

Because she didn't work full time, Amy had plenty of time to work on her book. She started immediately and worked tirelessly on it. Because Dale had not yet stopped running around at night, he was hardly there to ask what she was doing. After months of writing and editing, she sent the book off and awaited a response from the publishers. One day, she came home to a letter from a major publishing house that stated her book was going to be published. She felt a sense of accomplishment like none other that day. Everything her husband had taken from her was returned with that success. Because she was unknown, the book didn't hit any bestseller lists, but it did well enough for Amy to know that she had made a difference.

4

Even with the little bit she made from her book sales, Dale and Amy's financial situation did not improve in the next year. Dale was constantly searching for a better-paying job, but he had no success. Amy had even begun working every day in the real estate office, but between their location out in a rural community and the economy in a rough spot, everything moved at a crawl if it even moved at all, so she was not bringing home much herself. Amy brought the idea of moving to Oklahoma City up again so that they might both have better opportunities, but when they sat down and actually discussed it, the two decided that they didn't want to lose the equity they had in their house.

"This is about all we have left," Dale said as they talked about the possibility of moving. "This house is really our only investment."

"I guess you're right," Amy said pensively.

"I am," Dale assured her. "And the house in the city will cost more, so we'd just basically lose anything we'd saved. And we don't even know if we would do better off there, anyway."

"I would hate to move Andy now too," Amy added. "He's been doing so well, and the bullying has finally stopped. I guess I would've hated to move my junior year of school when I was a kid."

"I think that decides it then," Dale said finally. "We'll just have to keep our eyes peeled and our feelers out."

Although Amy knew that Dale meant to keep their feelers out for local job opportunities, she started to look into real estate all over the country. As much as Dale insisted things would get better and a job would come along, she could see that they were in dire need of a new plan, as Dale's had never worked out in the seventeen years they had been married. She persistently checked real estate in other parts of the country and kept her eyes open for any great deal. Without telling her husband, Amy had resolved to moving anywhere if she found something that she knew could finally create a better life for her family. She realized fully it would be a hard sale if it came to it since it had taken her husband sixteen years just to let her work, but she was resolute in making a big change if the opportunity presented itself. She also found subtle ways to make sure Andrew would not be devastated with a move. When he said on more than one occasion, "I think it'd be pretty cool to start over somewhere," Amy knew that a move was the right thing to do.

As she perused real estate listings from coast to coast, she highlighted any that appeared promising. There was a ranch in Oregon for sale. The place was gorgeous and had endless possibilities for development and resale, but the land was much too high for them even if they invested all the equity they had in their home. She marked the Oregon ranch off and continued on, until finally one day, she came across it— the perfect piece of land.

As she sat at her desk one soggy April afternoon, she came across a piece of land for sale in Florida that was actually in her price range. It was a sizable chunk of land near the everglades, and the description sounded wonderful.

> Large piece of waterfront land in very fertile area of south Florida. Land is surrounded by orange groves and away from the chaos of the city. Available land is 360 acres. Willing to split down to ten acre lots or at a discounted price if bought in full. Ideal for large development—can be zoned as residential or commercial.

She printed off the information about the land and emailed the link to her personal email to be sure she wouldn't lose it. As she read over the details and triple-checked her math to be sure the price was as low as she was figuring, she felt a surge of optimism course through her body. For the first time in years, she felt that perhaps her life was going somewhere; she felt that the life she wanted for her family may actually be in her grasp after nearly two decades of struggling.

When Amy got home from work that night, she could hardly mask the overwhelming enthusiasm she felt about the opportunity that had just presented itself. There it was—a piece of property that they could afford. It was a blank canvas for them to do whatever they wanted with it. This was their shot at finally getting ahead. All she had to do was convince Dale to take a chance on it.

Amy made Dale's favorite meal for dinner that night to prepare him for what she was about to ask. When he got home, she had chicken fried steak, homemade mashed potatoes, fried okra, and creamy county gravy waiting for him. She also picked up a six-pack of his favorite beer while she was out. She knew that she needed to do all she could to put him in a receptive mood, as he was not a fan of doing anything he did not dream up himself. He had already discarded the idea of moving just an hour away to Oklahoma City, so she was going to have to work hard to persuade him that Florida was the place for them.

"What's the occasion?" Dale asked suspiciously when he saw the spread laid out on the kitchen table. "Oh shit, did I forget our anniversary again?"

"No, hon, you didn't," Amy started. "I actually have some good news I want to share, and I thought I should make a special meal for it."

"Oh yeah?" he said, cracking open a Heineken. "What's that? Did you make a big sale finally? It's about damn time," he murmured as he grabbed a fork and plopped into his chair.

"I thought we could talk after dinner." She smiled sadly. "I'll call Andrew in to eat, and then I'll tell you."

"You're not pregnant are you?" he asked with a smirk. "I have noticed you've been a little sensitive lately."

"No, Dale, I'm not pregnant," she rolled her eyes.

The family had dinner that night and when Andrew disappeared to the office to play Call of Duty, Amy took a deep breath and pitched her idea.

"So, I found a piece of land that looks like a dream come true for us," she said as she grabbed the paper she'd printed off from her purse.

"For us?" Dale asked. "I thought you were selling property, not buying it."

"Well, I was, but I came across this," she said as she handed the paper to her husband. "And I thought…"

"This is in Florida, Amy," Dale blurted as he put his beer down hard on the table so that all the dished rattled in their places. "We can't move to Florida. Even if it was next door, we have no money. It's like you don't get what's going on, Amy."

"We would have money if we sold the house," she said as she scooted close to Dale.

"Sell the house, Amy?" Dale glared and shook his head. "We've talked about this. And we also said we don't want to tail Andy away from…"

"I know we have, babe. I know we said that we wanted to stay, but this place is a steal. I looked up property values in the area and they are practically giving it away.

"There must be a reason," Dale said, staring at the paper.

"They need to sell it, and they want to sell it whole so they don't have to mess with deeding it out piece by piece."

"What about Andrew? And school?" Dale asked, setting the paper down.

"He said he'd be okay with a move," Amy said hopefully, trying to gauge her husband's mood.

"So you talked to him about this and not me?"

"No, I didn't. I just have been feeling him out about it without telling him anything, and he told me he thought moving to a new place would be cool."

"I'm sure in theory, he does. If we get there and the school is full of asshole kids then…"

"I looked up the school already. It's called Middletown High School and it is in Middleton, Florida. They have small classes and very good teachers. It has great reviews and would actually be better than where he is. It isn't too big, but it's big enough that he would have more choices. I think he'd actually like it better there."

Dale stared down at the piece of paper and thought. He could see Amy was excited, but he decided that it was likely some fleeting idea she had. He knew that if he said a solid no, she would get mopey or keep pushing it. He figured if he just entertained the idea, she would lose interest and the whole thing would disappear.

"Let's just think about it," he said. "You know that I'm not crazy about selling the house, so let's just give it some thought."

Amy did give the idea more thought. In fact, it was all she thought and talked about. Dale could see that she was not letting this go. When she started planning out moving dates and figuring out how much to list the house for, he realized she was dedicated to her little plan. He acted like he didn't notice her preparations, still hoping that would discourage her, but she was persistent. Amy wasn't lost on his lack of enthusiasm. Everything she ever wanted to do, he had been opposed to, but she was set on this. This time, she would not back down and give Dale his way without a fight, and so she went ahead with the planning as if he had said yes.

During the next two weeks, Amy checked their finances, which was basically only the equity they had in their house, and the minuscule savings account that hovered at a thousand dollars and never seemed to move. Although their savings wasn't much, because of the large down payment they made on their house when they bought it seventeen years before, she figured that they could easily put the money down on the land and have enough left over to move to Florida. They wouldn't be able to live lavishly, but they never really had, so she didn't mind that.

"We can do this, Dale," she told him once she had everything calculated and planned out to a tee.

"Amy, this is all we have. You are asking me to sell all we have and move off to the swamps when I didn't even want to go to Oklahoma City," he told her one night while they got ready for bed.

"I know, Dale, but we will be finally comfortable once we do this," she told him. "What do we have to lose, Dale?"

"Our home!" he countered, his voice raised and his neck tense.

"Worst case scenario is we make just a little bit of money and we start over in a new place. I'm okay with that."

"And what if I'm not? This is my life too, Amy. I don't know how I got kicked out of it."

"I know it is, but what's here, Dale? There are no jobs. It's a town that talks about us because of what's gone on in the past, with a school that barely prepares our son for college."

"Our home is here, and our friends," Dale argued.

"What friends? The ones who spread rumors about us? The ones who promised you'd be a VP and then let you go? We can buy another home. We can start fresh," she insisted. "We can go to a place where everyone doesn't look at me like a fool because…" Amy stopped herself, knowing that if she went too far, Dale would become defensive and belligerent.

"And if we fall on our faces, we'll be all alone out there," Dale hissed back.

"Look, Dale," Amy said with ferocity in her hazel eyes. "I've always gone along with you—always. We have always done everything you wanted to do. I didn't work; I raised our son; I did whatever you said. This one time I'm asking, please give me a chance here."

Dale sat and contemplated what Amy said. He had half a mind to say no just because she had drudged up everything he had done wrong, but something strange came over him. He saw things from her point of view for the first time since they had been married. He also saw that they really hadn't gone anywhere. He would never admit that to anyone aloud, but she was right. They had no reason to stay there and drown. Besides, if they went and failed, he could remind Amy of it for the rest of their lives, and he would too.

"Okay then," he reluctantly agreed. "This is on you though. We're going to uproot our lives, so you better be right."

"It will be better for us," she promised. "I already figured it all out and we'll be ready to leave in a month. There are actually already two families interested in the house, so we'll just see who has the better offer."

"A month?" Dale shook his head. "We're gonna gamble it all in a month then?"

"This is going to be the best thing we ever did, babe," Amy said self-assuredly.

"It better be," Dale grumbled.

It was mid-April, so they decided to wait until the school year ended to take off. Luckily that worked out for them. The couple who bought their house had a lease to fulfill anyway, so they could wait until the end of May to move. While they waited for the school year to end, Amy arranged the purchase of the land and bought a small travel trailer for the family to stay in on the land while they put it on the market and waited for the money to come in.

"It's just temporary until we can build our own home." She smiled as she showed Dale and Andrew pictures of the mobile home.

The end of May rolled around, and Andrew said goodbye to his small group of friends. He was a little sad to leave but also excited about living in Florida. Because they had no money, the family never traveled, so it would be his first time to see Florida, or anywhere else for that matter. He also had his mom take him out to say good-bye to his wrestling coach, whom he had continued to practice with since they had started. With that, the family took off with their worldly possessions crammed into the modest travel trailer and a small U-haul that they hooked to the back of the family car. Amy drove their car and Dale piloted the massive RV, which pulled his small pickup behind it. There they were, headed down the road to Florida.

5

The Glades spent three days on the road, stopping each evening as the sun disappeared to greet the other side of the world. Amy had made reservations at the least expensive motels she could find along the way that were still in decent areas along the highway. She kept the paper she had printed out with the property information tucked away in her purse and pulled it out often to look at it. *This is our future*, she'd think as she studied the paper. On the third day, when the family finally made it to their destination, Amy felt her heart stop in her chest—but not in a good way—as they pulled onto their land.

"Are you kidding me?" Dale ranted as the three stepped out of their vehicles and surveyed the land. "Tell me there's been a mistake. Tell me you didn't just do this, Amy!"

Amy fumbled around in her purse frantically and pulled out the paper with all the information on it. She rushed to the car to get the sight-unseen deed as well. She read and reread the directions the previous owner had given her. There had been no mistake; they were on their property. Amy's ribs felt as tight as a boa constrictor around her lungs, and her skin tingled as she realized what had happened. There she stood on her very own 360 acres of land. Unfortunately, 300 acres of that land was underwater. Amy had talked her husband into purchasing a swamp.

"I just can't believe…" Amy said as she raised a hand to her mouth in shock.

"Well, believe it, because here we are," Dale snorted. "I should've known that letting you call the shots would lead to this. You didn't ask the guy if the land was usable, Amy?"

"It didn't say anything about this. I read and reread the description. Why would I think it was underwater?" she protested. "Why wouldn't someone tell…"

"Because if something looks too good to be true, then it probably is," he said in a mocking tone. "You are about as good at buying land as you are at selling it."

With that, they found a dry piece of the land that had a few shade trees and parked the travel trailer on the edge of a swampy area. Dale could see the disappointment and bewilderment on his wife's face, so he decided that he would stop antagonizing her for the time being. He realized that he too could have asked a few questions before buying the land, but he wasn't about to admit that out loud or let that fact steal from his anger toward his wife. Still, he fumed because they wouldn't be in the place they were had it not been for Amy.

"I guess we got a pig in a poke," he said as they stared out on the land. "Well, *you* did."

"I guess *we* did," Amy said, staring unblinkingly out at the water.

"Well, there's nothing to do for now since everything is closed, but we'll see what we can do to get our money back tomorrow and head back home," Dale said as he bounded up the collapsible stairs into the trailer.

When Dale disappeared into the trailer, Andrew walked over to his mother and stood quietly beside her for a few moments, looking out on the swamp that they now owned. He had been off throwing clods of dirt out into the murky water as his parents talked; he was just close enough to catch everything that was said. The boy felt his pulse quicken and his ears burn red-hot as he thought about the way his dad had just talked to his mom. Once he was standing by his mother, he caught a glance of her out of the corner of his eye and saw the disappointment and pain on her face, and his chest tightened. He couldn't understand why his father had to be so cruel to everyone all the time, or how he never felt guilty for destroying everyone around him.

"I'm so sorry, sweetie," Amy whispered, breaking the silence. A tear rolled down her face.

"Sorry for what, Mom?" Andrew asked, looking at his mother. Her apology stabbed him in the heart, and the burning in his ears moved to his face. The very realization that his mother was the one apologizing drudged up intense resentment in Andrew for his father. His muscles went rigid with anger and his guts felt like they were holding hot lava.

"For dragging us out here like this and getting us into this mess," Amy's voice quivered as she thought about how much she had let her family down—mostly Andy. "I took you away from your school and your friends. I uprooted you and look at this," she cried as she held her hands out toward the swamp.

"Don't let him take this from you, Mom," Andrew said, and Amy could hear the intensity in her son's voice. She was taken aback by Andrew's words and tone. He sounded like such an adult all of a sudden. It felt as if their roles had been switched and she was the teen and Andy the parent, giving advice and encouraging her.

"What do you mean, Andy?"

"I mean we shouldn't go back, Mom. Don't let him make you. He's bullying you right now, just like he always has. Stand your ground. Tell him no."

"Oh, sweetie, I wish it were that easy," Amy sighed.

"It can be, Mom. I'm here for you. No matter what he says, I'm here for you. Just like you were there for me when I was getting messed with," Andrew said as he tuned his body so that he was standing face-to-face with his petite mother. He locked eyes with her and said, "You taught me to fight back, Mom. Now it's time that you do the same. Don't let him intimidate you. You have always done everything he said, but it's time for you to stand up for yourself. You can do this; I know you can. I believe in you."

"Oh, Andy," Amy's voice cracked as she stepped forward and wrapped her arms around her son. "You are an amazing guy, you know that?" she said as she stepped back and looked at her son standing there before her, a man now instead of a boy.

"I wouldn't be without you." He smiled. "You are amazing too, Mom. And he just takes it for granted like he does everything. Let's stay here. You'll prove him wrong, I know you will. What would we do back in Oklahoma, anyway? What has he ever done that was so great?"

"You think so?"

"I know it, Mom. You can do this. *We* can do this."

"You don't want to go back to Oklahoma?"

"No way. This is our chance, Mom. I can make new friends. Just fight back, the way you taught me."

Amy smiled, hugged her son one more time, and wiped the tears away from her eyes. She looked out at the swampland again, took a deep breath, and then headed for the RV, where she knew Dale was sulking or throwing a fit. She realized that Andy was right. She never followed her heart; never stood up and spoke her mind if Dale snuffed out a dream. She had always been submissive, trapped in by Dale's bitterness and insecurity. She had spent the last decades under his thumb, letting him call all the shots, which had gotten them nowhere in life. It was time to slip her way out from beneath that crushing, suffocating force and follow her gut.

"We're not leaving for Oklahoma," Amy announced as she walked into the trailer, her tiny fists balled. She closed the door and stood at the top of the three stairs that led up into the tiny living area of the RV. There she planted herself. She was an Oak and she would not be moved.

"Excuse me?" Dale snapped as he stood up from the miniature kitchenette set he had been sitting at, working on his second beer.

"We're not going back," she said firmly. It was the first time in her life Amy stood up to Dale. The foreignness of it made her skin feel as if it were about to peel right off her bones.

"Like hell we aren't," he said, stomping over to Amy so that he was breathing his stale Coors Light breath right into her nostrils. "You got us into this, but that doesn't mean you're gonna hold us hostage in it. We're getting our money back and going back to Oklahoma where we never should've left in the first place!"

"We're staying," she said with a wince.

"We are in a bigger mess now than we have ever been in our lives because of this little stunt, Amy," he seethed. "And we are not staying here."

Andrew had moved closer to the travel trailer so he would be able to tell what was going on inside. He knew that his tyrant of a father would not likely take Amy's newfound assertiveness very well, and he would be there just in case things escalated too quickly. He stood, his ears pricked toward the trailer like a buck listening for the footsteps of approaching hunters. When Andrew heard his father's voice getting loud inside the RV, he swung the flimsy aluminum door open with a vengeance. He was tired of his father's temper, and he wasn't going to listen to it anymore.

Andrew looked up past his mother to lock his eyes on Dale, who was nearly toe-to-toe with Amy at that point. There his father stood, his eyes shining a blue brighter than the Pacific, the way they always did when he was angry. His face was the color of a cherry tomato, and his veins were bulging. Andrew started to step up into the RV to stand between his mother and father, but Amy stopped him before he could.

"Andrew, hon, why don't you go look around to see what the land looks like?" Amy said to her son, whose eyes were fixed on Dale.

"I think that maybe I'll stay here" Andrew said. "I've already seen the land anyway."

"Well, then why don't you take the main road into town and get us something to eat?" Amy suggested. She knew what Andrew was trying to do and it warmed her heart, but she didn't want her son to witness whatever came next in her and her husband's standoff.

"You're gonna let me drive the car?" he asked as he finally turned to face his mother. He hardly ever got to drive by himself, even though he had his license for almost a year. This was a big deal. As much as he wanted to drive, however, he was torn about whether or not he trusted leaving his mom there to face his dad alone.

"Yes sir," Amy said. She was leery about letting him drive in a new place, but she could feel that it was best that Andrew leave at the moment.

"Are you sure?" Andrew asked, looking at Amy and then Dale and back to Amy again.

Amy nodded and forced a reassuring smile. When she could see that Andrew was still making no signs of moving, she put a hand on Andrew's back, leading him out of the RV. She pushed the door closed and walked her son out far enough from the trailer, where she knew Dale wouldn't overhear the two of them.

"Honey, I'll be fine, I promise," she said in a hushed voice. "You go and grab some dinner so I can talk to Dad."

"Are you sure, Mom?"

"Sweetie, he may be a jerk, but I can handle it. He's all bark and no bite, okay? You go and let us talk. Take advantage of getting a little freedom, okay?" She smiled.

"If you're sure," he said, taking the keys that Amy had been holding between the two of them.

Once Andrew was out of sight, Amy turned around, stormed back into the trailer, and let loose eighteen years of pent-up anger. They went on to have the biggest fight in their married life. Neither would back down. Dale was almost too shocked at his wife's insolence to react at first, but he quickly recovered and jumped in, claws retracted and ready to tear flesh. Dale shouted about how Amy had wrecked everything for them and told her it was a mistake ever listening to her. Amy countered his attacks by reminding him that if he'd been a better provider in the first place, they wouldn't even be there to begin with.

"Maybe if you were as concerned with our well-being as you are with messing around, getting drunk, and picking up strippers, we'd be back in Oklahoma living it up!"

"You don't even know what you're talking about," Dale growled.

"I do the laundry, Dale. I see where you go on receipts that are left behind, you son of a bitch," she spat. She had actually known of several affairs and one-night stands of his but had only mentioned one when she realized he would never change or regret anything he did anyway. She wasn't being quiet anymore, however.

"If you would do your job, I wouldn't have to go looking around in bars!" Dale boomed.

"Oh, I'm sure, Dale. Because nothing is Dale Glade's fault, is it? God forbid the great American athlete realize he's not a hot shot anymore and learn to take care of his business."

The two went on like that until Andrew returned with Popeye's chicken. They held their tongues for the rest of the night and did not even look at one another. They went to bed still infuriated. Dale slept in his tiny truck; he was so outraged by their fight and the predicament they were in. Amy cooled off as the night went on and even felt bad for some of the things she had said, even if she knew she was right about all of them. Dale, however, only seemed to get hotter.

The next morning, Amy suggested that they go into town and check around to see what was happening in the area before they made any drastic decisions. Dale was baffled that she was still insisting that they stay. She had never been so defiant before, and he did not appreciate it.

"If we go to town, it'll be to find a divorce attorney," he said, with Andrew sitting just feet away.

"What?" Amy asked.

"If you want to stay here so bad, you can do it by yourself," Dale said, his jaw set and his eyes shining intensely through the slits he was glaring out of. "I'm leaving here, with or without you."

"That's your choice then," she said, trying to keep her voice steady.

Dale left that day and, true to his word, found someone to start the divorce papers. He couldn't head back to Oklahoma just yet, as they had to work out all the details and have the papers filed first. As the two sat in a room with an attorney, they split everything they owned. They agreed that Amy would receive all the land, the trailer, her car, and custody of Andrew. Dale would get his truck and most of what was left of the savings they had, which was about a thousand dollars—enough money to get out of town and put first month's rent down somewhere back in Oklahoma. As soon as they had signed off on everything, Dale gathered up what was his and left his ex-wife and son on the swamp. Andrew stayed quiet through it all and hardly looked at his father as he packed his things.

The day after, Dale left Amy, and Andrew drove into town to the high school so Andrew could see the campus and they could meet with the principal—a tall, lean woman named Mrs. Stidham, with salt-and-pepper hair and large, inquisitive, but kind, eyes. The school seemed nice, much nicer than Andrew's last school, as did Mrs. Stidham and the couple of teachers who happened to be there for a summer program, which made Amy feel better about her decision. The football coach, a man in his early thirties named Derek Roberts, who was made of bundles of tightly wound muscles and polyester, particularly stuck out to Andrew.

Coach Roberts was the last person Andrew talked to before he left, and he immediately took to the coach. Andrew had never played football before, but as the coach rested a hefty paw on Andrew's shoulder and told him how the football team was like a family there in Middletown, football suddenly had an appeal to the boy whose father had just skipped town. The coach, though a bit intimidating in his muscular stature, wore an eternal smile. The smile he wore pushed his dark brown eyes nearly closed, so it looked as if he were constantly squinting; at the corners of his eyes were permanent lines etched into his skin that stood as proof that his smile hardly ever faded. Andrew had always equated manhood with austerity because of his father. Seeing the football coach wink and grin was a welcome relief to the boy.

"Did ya play football back at home, Andy?" the coach asked.

"No, sir," Andrew replied sheepishly, desperately wishing he could have answered yes just to please the coach.

"Well, it's never too late to start!" He chuckled. "If you want to, that is. There's a lot of great stuff to do outside of football, but I am a little biased about it. If you're up to it, I think it'd be a great way to get to know some great kids," he said.

"I *have* wrestled," Andrew chirped.

"Is that right?" Coach Robertson said. "I hate to say we don't have much of a wrestling team. Maybe you could carry what you know about wrestling into football though, right?" The coach smiled.

"Okay then," Andrew replied hopefully. "Maybe."

"There will be a camp in just three weeks if you decide you're interested. It'll be down at the community college," he added.

Coach Roberts went on to tell Amy a bit more about the football team and his philosophy on sports. Although Amy was a little relieved when her son showed no interest in an activity that required a lot of smashing and hard blows to the body from other 160-plus-pound players, the way the coach discussed teamwork and a sense of unity made her reconsider her ideas about football. She also liked that the coach made it a point to say that he had a strict no-bullying code in place that all his players knew not to test.

"Football players get a pretty bad rap these days for being bullies," he said, and his smile nearly faded for the first time since he started talking. "It's kind of my mission to help change that in any way I can. I want my boys to do the opposite—to stand up to bullies, not do the bullying."

"That's…that's amazing," Amy said, almost moved to tears.

"That's how it should be," Coach Roberts smiled. "Well, I guess I better get to the field house now. You have a good day, and welcome to Middletown," the coach said as he headed off.

"Well, what do you think, kiddo?" Amy asked as they walked to the car.

"It's pretty cool," he said. "The coach is pretty awesome. I think I may try out for football," he said as he stared back toward the football stadium that stood towering behind them like Oz.

"Not a bad idea," Amy said, throwing one arm over her son's shoulders as they walked.

After they had toured the school, they went to the community center in the middle of the town to ask about the land they had just bought. There at the center, Amy talked to a man at the information desk who looked to have just enough muscle left to keep him upright. He had skin so thin you could see the blue veins beneath it and wispy white hair that looked like the tufts of a dandelion atop his bobbing head. Both his hair and his body looked as if they might blow away if someone were to sneeze in his vicinity.

"Excuse me," Amy said to the man. "Do you know about this property?" she asked, sliding him the paper.

The man adjusted his thick glasses that weighed heavy on his bulbous nose and pulled the paper to his eyes.

"I'm sure I do." He smiled. "Lived here my whole life."

Amy smiled and nodded as the man examined the paper. He finally put the paper down and said, "I know all about the property. It's been sold three times in the last five years, to gullible folks who buy it sight-unseen."

"I guess I make it four then," Amy frowned.

"My apologies, Miss," the man said, a little embarrassed. His pasty grey complexion flushed a slight pink, almost hiding some of his liver spots.

"Oh, you're fine," she said. "I guess now I just have to come up with a new plan."

"Good luck," he said as Amy walked away.

Amy let Andrew drive home that day as she contemplated their next move. She wasn't going to do what someone had done to her and deceive anyone else into buying the land; that much she knew. What she couldn't quite figure out though was what to do to honestly make money off the swamp she owned.

6

The idea of a football camp clung tight to Andrew's mind like a goat-head sticker to a cotton sock for days after they had talked to the coach. He hadn't ever played football, but he had made strides in wrestling and he began to think that if he joined the football team, he might be able to show the other guys things he had learned from James to help on the football field. Not only would that help him adjust to the new school; it would make the coach proud, which was a longing that had strangely gripped Andrew within the first few moments of meeting the muscle-bound man. If he could just get to that camp, then he would have a shot at sharing his wrestling knowledge. He knew, though, that paying for football camp was outside of their means at the time. That thought distressed the teen, and his mother could see that something was nagging at her son.

"What's going on, kiddo?" she asked over dinner one night, when she could see that her son had been picking at his food and aloof. She assumed it had to do with the divorce and his father leaving.

"Oh, I dunno," he said. He could feel the words jumbled and knotted together at the back of his throat. He grappled with whether or not he should let them out.

"I know the divorce and all this change is hard, sweetie," Amy started. "And I am here for anything you need to talk about. I mean that."

Andrew sat silent for a few minutes, his stomach churning while the words lodged themselves in his throat. He wanted to tell his mom what was really bothering him but didn't want to put more stress on her. He felt overwhelmed by the conflicting feelings, and Amy saw the strain in his eyes.

"Andy, I'm your mom. It's my job to help. Let me."

"I just wanted to go to that dumb camp I guess," he blurted, forcing the wad of words out in a giant exhale.

"The football camp?"

"Yeah, but I know it's not something we have money for."

"So you want to play football?"

"Yeah. It's just the coach is so…"

"He is pretty great, isn't he?"

"Yeah, like he's not what you think of when you think of jocks and stuff. And I just thought I could get to know the guys on the team and be a part of something here or something. I dunno…"

"Andy, we'll get you to that camp," Amy said, reaching her hand out to her son.

"No, Mom. I know we don't have…'

"I'm Mom, Andy. We will make it," she said. "I will find the money."

The next day, Amy and Andrew went up to the school and signed Andrew up for football camp. While Andrew looked over the schedule, Amy talked to Coach Roberts about all that Andrew would need and explained their financial situation.

"I've got plenty of equipment," the coach said. "He can use my extras for camp, so don't worry about that. What's his size?"

Amy gave the coach Andy's shoe size and measurements. The coach jotted them down on an aqua-blue sticky note and assured her that all Andrew needed to show up with was underwear, socks, and himself. As they were finishing up talking, Andrew walked up to the two.

"If you think it could help, I could come up here and show the guys some wrestling moves that might help," Andrew told the coach. "I had a really great coach back home, and I'd do it for free."

"You know what, I think that sounds like a pretty good idea," the coach said after thinking it over. "We've had a rough few seasons, so I'll give anything a try."

"Really?" Andrew asked hopefully.

"I just have to run it by the principal and get some waivers written up for everyone. We wouldn't start yet, but if the principal okays it, we can do it during gym when school starts up."

"Awesome," Andrew beamed.

"I'll let you know at camp what the principal says."

The next two and a half weeks took an eternity to pass for Andrew. While he jogged and did squats to prepare for camp, Amy started researching ways to remove water from land and also snuck off to pawn her wedding ring so she could pay for camp. The day Andrew was set to leave finally arrived and when he got to the school, the coach was waiting with brand new cleats, football socks, and workout gear for Andrew that the coach had bought with his own money. When Andrew asked where all the stuff came from, the coach answered, "This will be in exchange for the wrestling class you are going to help teach. Now I don't want to hear another word, because you will earn all of it, son."

So off to camp Andrew went, where he got to know all the other football players. All of the guys seemed more than welcoming, with the exception of a couple standoffish boys who glared at the new kid every time they passed him. Andrew didn't let the couple of bad apples distract him though. He worked with his team, who cheered him on as he took to running plays and handling the ball. He had played plenty of backyard football, so he wasn't a complete neophyte.

He actually seemed to take naturally to the sport, which impressed both his coach and teammates.

When Andrew returned from camp, he appeared to be a new kid. Amy saw something in him she hadn't in some time. He held his head higher and his eyes burned bright when he talked about the team and how well he did. He could hardly wait for school to start, which was a godsend to Amy, who was terrified he would not adjust to their new life well. He had also met at the camp another kid his age named Gabe Mulroy who he talked endlessly about.

"I think I'm gonna go stay the weekend with him if that's cool so we can work on some plays and workout together," he said excitedly over dinner.

"That sounds great, kiddo." Amy smiled. "But I do want to meet his parents first."

"Yeah, no problem. His dad's name is Jerry. He's like some kind of engineer for the army or something. I met him when he picked Gabe up, and he seems cool. Gabe says he's awesome."

"What about his mom?"

"She's not really around. They got divorced when Gabe was a little kid, and I guess she kind of just went off and did her own thing."

"That's too bad," Amy frowned. "Poor guy."

"Nah, he's cool with it. His dad is cool enough for two parents, he says, just like you." Andrew smiled at his mom.

Amy met Jerry and Gabe that evening over dinner at the Mulroys' house and gave her stamp of approval. As the boys played video games and skateboarded out on the driveway, Amy and Jerry got acquainted with one another. Amy was surprised at how easy it was to talk to Jerry, considering he was both a man and a stranger. She had come to see men as a bit antagonistic and berating after Dale. Jerry was anything but.

"Andrew mentioned you are an engineer," Amy said as they sipped coffee together.

"Yes, ma'am," Jerry replied. "I work for the US Army Corp of Engineers. I went into the army right out of high school, then went to college on the government's dime, honing what the army had started with engineering. I was always a bit of a math nerd, and it happened that engineering loves math nerds," he chuckled softly.

"That is so neat," Amy said.

"I don't think I've heard what you do," Jerry said.

"Oh, I just do some clerical work now. I did dabble in real estate, but apparently I'm no good at that. I have a degree in creative writing, but that isn't so practical, I'm finding. I did get published once though."

"That's amazing. What kind of book?"

"A fiction, young adult book about bullying. I based it on Andy somewhat."

"Well, I'd say that is quite an accomplishment," he said.

"Oh, I suppose I am proud of it, but it doesn't do much to pay the bills. That's why I dabbled in real estate. That is obviously not paying the bills either, though. I have a useless swamp and no savings now," she said jokingly, but there was a hint of defeat in her laugh.

"Don't be so hard on yourself," he told her. "I'm sure you'll find a way to make it work."

"I plan to." She smiled.

The Glades and the Mulroys continued to get to know each other over the rest of the summer. Gabe and Andrew became the best of friends, and so Jerry and Amy also became better acquainted. The two boys spent most of their time playing football, exploring the town, or messing around on the swamp that Amy had bought. They still had almost two months of summer vacation, so they met with Coach Roberts to ask him if there was anything they could do during the summer months to be sure they got a spot on the varsity team in the fall. The football camp had ignited a fire within both of them, and they wanted nothing more than to start as the running back and quarterback come fall.

"Well boys, I hate to say it, but I already have a quarterback and a running back in line for the coming year...you can certainly come to try out for it, though. Who knows?"

"Oh, we will," Gabe promised.

Gabe had developed quite a strong arm, and Andrew found out at camp that he was well-coordinated and quick, so the coach told them to just keep practicing, which they did all summer, and be there for tryouts at the beginning of the school year.

Amy was relieved to see that Gabe didn't mind at all where Andy lived. She had worried at first that Andrew might be picked on for living in an RV on a swamp, but was glad to see that Gabe thought the arrangement was awesome and actually liked coming out to stay with them on their land.

"It's like the best camping ever," he said one night as they were watching a sci-fi movie in the RV after dark.

When the summer finally came to an end, Andy started the school year with a best friend. He also started his wrestling practices with both the football team and the kids who wanted to play a sport but weren't keen on football. Within a week, everyone had heard of the wrestling class, and it got so big that they had to have the practice after school when Andrew was finished with football. Andrew would take his pads off and then head inside the field house to work with the wrestlers on bodybuilding and weight lifting to increase their upper body strength. Wrestling got so popular that the coach and principal decided that they would form a wrestling team that year to compete against other high schools in the area.

Although Andrew loved to help with wrestling, he found that he loved football just as much. Both he and Gabe had dedicated themselves to football for the entire summer, determined to earn their spots as quarterback and running back. They knew that they had to fight hard to get the positions they wanted. Because Andrew was new and Gabe had not started the year before, they knew it wasn't going to be easy, but neither would back down. It was a tough battle and they had to work hard, but both had begun to believe in themselves. Amy had sparked something great in Andrew when she took him to learn how to wrestle, and that spark was contagious and growing into a burning flame.

When their first football game rolled around the second week of school, Gabe walked onto the field as first-string quarterback and Andrew as the running back. Andrew had always thought his size would keep him from being any good at football. As it turned out, however, his smallness and agility worked perfectly for a running back. The team won their first game against an infamous private school that everyone believed recruited players—it was a team they had not beaten in several years and had become a huge rival. Jerry and Amy sat side by side, cheering their boys on to victory. Amy knew how hard Andrew fought, not just for the win, but for his place on the team. She beamed with pride when the final horn blew and Andrew looked up and waved before disappearing off the field. She hoped with all her heart that they had finally found their place.

7

Because she knew that it could be some time before she found an answer to the swamp problem, Amy got a job doing clerical work at the town hall to help pay the bills while she figured out what to do next. Although she was no better off than she was in Oklahoma, she felt that for the first time in her life, she was in control of her own fate, and that gave her confidence. She also saw Andrew thriving in his new school, which made her content regardless of their strained finances. Being married to Dale, she had become very accustomed to strained finances, anyhow.

It was Andrew's senior year that year, and he would be turning eighteen on September 21. Amy had promised Andrew since he got his license that he would get a car on his eighteenth birthday as long as he was doing well in school and staying out of trouble. It was September 12, and to date, Andrew had maintained a 3.5 GPA and was currently leading his football team. He had also created a wrestling team from nothing, which Amy knew earned him a car of his own.

Amy realized that anything she did, she would have to do on her own, as Dale had made it clear she would be getting no money since she had "lost" all they had in the swamp. Determined to stay true to her word, she went down to the local car dealer and worked out buying Andrew a car on credit. The salesman made her a deal that she wouldn't have to make a payment for ninety days. Although she knew it would put them in a tough place to take on another bill, she knew if she could just get the water off her land that she could pay the car off in no time. She hoped it didn't take much longer than the ninety days she was given.

And so Amy purchased a powder-blue 1994 Ford Taurus with a tape deck and automatic windows—not the sleekest or fastest car in the world, but something reliable that would get Andrew anywhere he wanted to go. It was nine days until Andrew's birthday, so Amy left it at the dealership and waited until the twenty-first, at which time she drove Andrew to the dealership blindfolded and presented him with his own car.

"Oh my gosh, Mom! Seriously?" he exclaimed when he saw his car.

"Seriously." She smiled. "I know it isn't a hot rod, but…"

"It's freakin' perfect," he interjected, wrapping his arms around his tiny mother. "It'll get the job done." He winked and then took the keys and slid into his "new" car.

As he turned the radio on and off and opened and closed the glove compartment, melancholy suddenly swept over him, and Amy could see his expression turn grave.

"What is it?" she asked, concerned. "You don't like it, do you?"

"It's not that at all…We can't afford this, Mom," he said. "This is so awesome, but—"

"We can," she cut him off. "I'm figuring out how to get the water off our land, hon. When we get rid of the water in the swampy area of the land, we can sell the lots one at a time for people to build houses on them. People are moving down in droves from New England, looking for a good place to live that has good weather."

"How do you know?"

"I've been doing nonstop research," she told him. "Just trust me. That land will go like hotcakes when we get that water off it."

Amy had done her research. She had priced land around them, looked at the selling trends over the last decade, and most importantly, she was wearing herself out looking for ways to drain the land. The first two were looking very promising; it was the issue of getting the water off the swamp that plagued her.

One possibility she found was simply filling in the area with massive amounts of fill dirt to raise the elevation of the land so that the water would drain off into the nearby swampland. That avenue was terribly expensive, however, and on doing a little more digging, she saw that most developers avoided land that had been created that way, as there was a tendency for the soil to sink over time and create massive structural issues. She remembered that there had actually been a pond in the Oklahoma City area that had been developed that way, but the main engineering firms in the area wouldn't touch it because of the risks of major catastrophes down the road.

When filling in the swamp brought her to a dead end, she started to look into draining it. In a place like Florida, the method of draining had been used for several locations. During her research, she found that if one could only get the money to do so, land that had been drained tended to be extremely fertile, making it perfect for development. The land would be ideal for anything from golf courses to farming. Draining it looked to be even more expensive than filling it in in some cases, however. It seemed that no matter what the solution may be, it would cost *a lot*.

Just days after Amy and Andrew celebrated his eighteenth birthday, Amy headed up to the local bank to present her idea in hopes of obtaining a loan that would help drain the property. Amy had spent hours preparing a plan, gathering research to prove her plan could work, and coming up with a pitch to convince a banker that her idea would pay off in the end. With her folders of statistics, research, and proposal in hand, Amy took off for the bank wearing her nicest business suit.

"Well, the draining could work," the overly-tanned banker with unnaturally blond hair said, looking at all of Amy's research and tapping a pen on his oak desk. "But the problem is, it also couldn't. And you have no assets to use as collateral if that happens," he said, with a frown on his leathery face.

"The land is my collateral," she said, scooting to the edge of her chair.

"If this doesn't work, that land is all but worthless," the banker told her matter-of-factly.

"But if it is drained, it will be worth much more. There's no way it wouldn't."

"Listen, Miss Glade. I understand that you got yourself in a bind here, but I just can't help you. There's no telling what'd be under all that water. It's just not a risk we're willing to take on."

"Thank you for your time, then," Amy said dejectedly as she gathered all her papers.

"I'm sorry, Miss Glade," the banker said as Amy walked out. Amy simply nodded her head and walked on. It was back to the drawing board for her.

8

With the added cost of Andy's car and the realization that it may take a little more time than she had intended to figure out how to get the water off her land so that she could actually make money on it, Amy decided she needed to be bringing in more income than she was with her clerical job. She went to town one morning and started hunting for something that would give them a bit more cash flow while she worked on the swamp issue. As luck would have it, there was a small real estate company that didn't need a full-time employee but was happy to hire Amy part-time.

"We could use you from eight to noon if that works," a woman named Shelly, with bleach blond streaks in her auburn hair and bronze skin, said, flashing an unnaturally white smile that shone against her red lipstick.

"That will work perfectly," Amy said. She figured she could work in the mornings and use the afternoons to continue working on getting the water off her land.

The next few weeks, after she got off at the real estate office, she travelled around the area to do some research on how to tackle her swamp. She found out that there were some other areas just like hers that had been nothing more than swamplands at one time, but the owners had the water removed. One of the areas had been turned into an orange grove, which became quite a profitable venture. The problem that she kept running into with every possible approach to draining her land, however, was money.

To make sure she approached the drainage issue best, she decided to go talk to the owners of one of the orange groves nearby to find out what worked best for them to get the water off their property. She had done plenty of internet research, but none of it had said how to best tackle Florida swamps. She figured that talking to someone who had been successful was the best kind of research she could possibly do. She felt optimism bubbling up inside her, starting at her toes and working up to the crown of her head, at the thought of talking to someone who had been able to get water off of land just like hers. *Why had I not thought of this before!* she wondered as she drove down a long, gravel drive that was lined with orange trees to talk to the grove owners about how they cleared their land.

The couple who owned the orange and lemon groves were named Tim and Marie Swanson. They were in their late forties and had the air of hardworking farmers about them, but seemed a little bohemian at the same time. They both wore denim overalls and rubber boots. Marie's ashy-blond hair was tousled from wearing a straw sun hat all day. They were both kind, but Tim was a bit on the quiet side, so Marie did most of the talking. She was a stout woman—muscular, not fat—with piercing green eyes and broad shoulders. Tim was almost the exact same build as his wife, only his shoulders were narrower. He wore his graying hair long, down to his shoulders, but kept it tied back in a ponytail.

"So you bought the swamp, didn't you?" Marie said as she poured Amy a cup of green tea. "I can't believe the crooks are selling that place without telling folks it's underwater."

"I should have known better, I guess," Amy said.

"People should be honest," Marie replied. "Everything is about money these days, and you aren't a good business person unless you have no qualms about lying."

"It's a shame," Tim added in a soft, low voice as he shook his head.

"Well, I'll tell you, one of the main reasons the swamp is there is because it is fed by a Keller ditch that is just above your land," Marie said, stirring her tea with her index finger.

"Really?" Amy said.

"Yes, ma'am. The first thing you'll have to do is divert the water from the Keller ditch to a different place."

"Is that what you all did?"

"It is," Marie nodded. "We had a lot of time, though, so I don't know if you'd want to take the same approach we did. Plus, it will depend on what you use the land for on how you want to go about it. You may want to talk to an engineer as well. That's what we did."

"I actually was planning to go do that at some point." Amy smiled. "Thanks so much for everything. I can't say how much this has meant to me. I feel like maybe there's hope after all."

"Don't give up." Marie smiled. "You can do this. If we did, so can you. You just have to put in the work."

"Oh, I plan to do that," Amy said as she got up from her chair and shook both Marie and Tim's hand. She noticed that Marie had a firm handshake, where Tim's hand felt like she was holding limp pasta noodles.

Each day, Amy spent hours doing research on ways to eliminate the water coming in from the ditch. Research on draining looked plausible, but she had to weed her way through the different methods to find one that would work for her. The first method she found was something called tubewell drainage. To do this, she would have to constantly control the water table of the swamp and use underground wells. The more she looked into this approach, the less possible it sounded to her, as it required a number of very specific conditions to actually work, including the type of soil and the hydrogeological conditions. Besides that, she read that it took a number of people to maintain this to keep the drainage going and that the people needed to be highly trained, which she was not. Most importantly, the practice was hardly done in the United States—she hit a dead end.

There was also something called a bedding system she came across, but that took years to actually get the water into one central place, and Amy did not have that kind of time. She went on to a technique she called a French drain, which, she had read, was also called a land drain. She found that to do a French drain, she'd need a number of massive plastic pipes and also equipment large enough to build huge ditches for the pipes. The problem with this technique was that it evenly distributed the water of the land, but she wanted to get rid of the water altogether.

She finally found something called mole drainage. Eureka! This was used on land that had no slope, just like her swamp, and it was great for very wet, heavy soil. The greatest part was it seemed to require the least materials—it was simply a huge unlined ditch dug by something called a ripper blade. All she needed was to get someone who could do it and had the equipment, and hope that the bank would reconsider her loan if she could get someone to tell them the land was usable.

9

At school, Andrew was becoming quite popular. His wrestling class had gotten so big that he could hardly keep up with it anymore. It had also grown to the point that not every kid in the class would actually get a spot on the wrestling team. When Andrew first proposed the class and having a team, he assumed that he'd be lucky to get enough people to even compete. Once it became all the rage and boys from freshmen to seniors were showing up daily, however, it became clear that his class was a double-edged sword; he had created something people loved on the one hand, but with so many people in the class, there would be some who were told they didn't make the cut when it came time to hit the tournaments.

Being the sensitive kid he was, Andrew knew he didn't have it in him to tell anyone they didn't have a spot on the team. That is when he got the idea of getting an actual wrestling coach. A real wrestling coach would help him both teach the enormous class and make the decision of who gets to suit up and who would be sitting on the sidelines when wrestling season came. Once he worked up the nerve, he went to Coach Roberts to ask him about his idea.

"Coach?" Andrew said as he walked slowly into the coach's office like a small child about to ask his mother for a cookie before dinner.

"Hey there, Andy! How goes it?"

"Good," Andrew answered nervously, staring at the stained carpet beneath his feet. "Um, I was just thinking that…" Andrew stopped as the words caught in his throat.

"Go on," the coach said, his famous smile there to encourage him.

"Well, you know the wrestling class has gotten really popular and all," he stammered. "And there's like tons of guys now…"

"I have noticed that. You did good thinking that up, Glade," Coach grinned.

"Well, I was just thinking…what do you think about us getting a wrestling coach? Since the class is so big now, I mean."

"Well, Andy, I don't know. We'd have to run it by Mrs. Stidham, you know. She's the principal, so she'd really be the one to help you out here."

"Yeah, I figured. It's just that the class is huge, and some of the guys are really good, you know. I think it'd be good to bring in an actual coach to help out—one who knows about wrestling and could maybe actually take the team somewhere when the wrestling season rolls around in a couple months."

"Well, I mean, I'm all for it, bud. We just have to get it okayed and all that."

"You think they will okay it?" Andrew probed.

"I don't see why not. We're doing pretty good with money, and it looks like a program people will like a lot. It'd do us good to have it."

"I hope so because I don't want to have to tell anyone they can't be on the team," Andrew sighed. "You know, with all the kids wanting to wrestle, I know people will have to be cut, and I just can't do that, you know? I mean, I like all those guys and—"

"Oh, I get ya, bud," Coach interrupted. "I hate it myself. I wish everyone could play. But you know, if we do get a coach, we can make a JV team, just like we do with football. That'd help give everyone some mat time."

"I never even thought of that," Andrew said, his face lighting up.

"Well, I guess that's why you need a coach to help out. They think of these things." Coach smiled, his brown eyes disappearing in the folds of his tan skin.

The next day, Coach Roberts and Andrew went to Mrs. Stidham and presented her with the idea of hiring a professional coach to help the kids with the wrestling class that had gotten so popular that it had nearly burst out of the walls of the field house. Andrew felt confident about asking this favor because he knew that wrestling was giving several boys who had never played a sport before the chance to be a part of something that not only gave them some muscle tone but also provided them with a feeling of unity. His class gave his peers a newfound sense of self, just like it had Andrew when he started years before.

"What about Jennings?" Mrs. Stidham asked after she thought about the request a moment.

Jennings was Coach Roberts's assistant. He was a tiny firecracker of a man wound so tightly that it seemed he could break in two at any moment. He was intense and quick about everything he did, but he had a heart so big that it barely fit in his five-foot-five-inch frame. The man had a passion for all he did, and that included coaching kids.

"You know, that's not a bad idea," Coach said, slumping back in his chair, lifting a giant paw to his bottom lip. "Jennings is great with the kids, and he actually wrestled a little in junior college. He's also dying to get on full-time."

"I'd say we have our solution then." Mrs. Stidham smiled. "Let me just run it by the superintendent. It will be much easier this way because we'll just be upping a current employee's hours."

"Sound good to you, Andy?" Coach asked with a wink.

"Yes, sir." Andy beamed. "Coach Jennings is great."

"I'll talk to Mrs. Glover and get back to you all by the end of the week. Keep your fingers crossed. Oh, and let's not make any announcements until we know, okay?" Mrs. Stidham added.

"You got it," Coach said, and he and Andrew thanked Mrs. Stidham and headed back for the field house. As they walked, Andrew barely felt his feet hitting the ground; he was so swept up by the idea of getting a real coach. He realized that he had started something great, and he hoped against hope that this would work out—not just for him, but for the whole team.

10

Although Andrew had promised he wouldn't say anything to anyone about the possibility of a real wrestling coach, he couldn't help but tell Gabe. Besides Andrew, Gabe was the most enthusiastic wrestler in the school and he couldn't keep such a huge secret from his best friend. After they finished football and wrestling practice the following day, try as he might to hold it back, Andrew let fly the news.

"Coach Jennings is probably gonna come on as a full-time wrestling coach," Andrew blurted as he drove to Gabe's house from school.

"Seriously?" Gabe asked.

"Seriously," Andrew repeated. "That way we'll have a coach when the season starts, and we can even have a JV team."

"Dude, that's awesome! I know we were pumped about the season, but I was wondering how we could do it without a real coach…an adult, I mean."

"Well, we have one now." Andrew grinned. "But keep it on the down low. We're still waiting to hear back for sure."

"Who am I gonna tell?" Gabe smiled.

"The school." Andy ribbed him.

"Psh, I can keep a secret." Gabe laughed. "Hey, you and your mom should totally come over to eat with us the night after we find out, to celebrate. I think my dad digs your mom anyway," Gabe joked.

"Shut up." Andy laughed. "But we will be there if you're serious. Tell your dad to grill steaks and I will *definitely* be there. We're living on mac and cheese and hamburger while my mom is working on trying to figure out how to sell the land," he said as he contorted his face and held his stomach as if he were about to throw up on the dashboard of his car.

"Dude, there's nothing wrong with easy mac and hamburger. That was like my favorite meal when I was five." Gabe smirked.

"Still, steak is better."

"I'll see what I can do."

That night, Gabe asked Jerry if they could have the Glades over for dinner on Saturday, even though he didn't know yet if they would have anything to celebrate or not. Gabe liked having Amy over for some reason. She seemed to make the house feel more complete the few times she was there. He also liked to see his dad with Amy; he seemed more relaxed around her. He had been spending all his time raising Gabe and working the last decade, so it was nice to see his dad simply enjoying the company of another adult.

"What do you think about having a little cookout with Amy and Andy Saturday night?" Gabe asked as Jerry flipped through the channels.

"That sounds pretty good, actually. What's the occasion?"

"I just thought it'd be nice. They're on a tight budget so I was thinking we could make them something good, like steak."

"I like the sound of a good steak." Jerry smiled. "Say, kiddo, why are they on such a tight budget?"

"Well, you know they live out on that swamp."

"Yes, but I thought that it was an investment," Jerry nodded.

"Well, I guess it is, but they still live out there in an RV because all Amy's money is tied up in that land that she can't sell. I guess Andy's dad is some kind of a deadbeat who just took off because he was mad that Amy bought it or whatever."

"So she doesn't get any help from Andy's dad?"

"I don't think so. Andy says if she can find a way to get the water out of there and sell it, they'll be rolling in dough, but she's got no money to do that. I don't want to tell him, but I don't see how they'll ever get the water off as long as Amy is so broke. They live on mac and cheese right now. There's no way they can pay for that."

"I see," Jerry said, leaning back in his recliner and staring past the television set. "That's a shame."

"Yeah, but they seem to get by. Plus I think the RV is awesome. It's like being on a trip or something all the time."

"You may think differently if you lived there," Jerry said.

"Probably." Gabe shrugged. "So Saturday?" he asked, changing the subject.

"Saturday it is. I'll get the biggest rib eyes I can find tomorrow." Jerry smiled, but he couldn't shake the thought of Amy and Andy out on that swamp in an RV all alone, eating macaroni and cheese. He felt a knot in his throat thinking about it.

Saturday rolled around, and Andy and Amy pulled up to the Mulroy's at six on the dot. They could smell the smoky, hickory scent of the grill in the still, warm Florida air as soon as they got out of their cars.

"Steak!" Andrew said in an excited whisper.

"It smells amazing," Amy said as she grabbed the pasta salad she had made for the cookout.

When they got to the front door, Gabe waved them in. "We're in the backyard," he said as he led Andy and Amy to the backyard where the grill was.

"It'll be ready in about ten," Jerry announced from his place in front of the grill. "There are some munchies on the table over on the deck, and some drinks. In the pitcher is margarita," he said to Amy.

"Wow," Amy said as she looked at the spread that consisted of bacon-wrapped jalapenos fresh from the grill, barbeque shrimp, a heaping bowl of homemade bean dip with chips, fired zucchini, and deviled eggs. "You did not have to do all this."

"Nah. I'm happy to. It gave me an excuse to make some of my favorites. Plus, I enjoy entertaining; I just never do it," Jerry said as he lifted his Corona to his lips.

Once dinner was ready, the four of them took their seats at the large table on their deck, which was shaded by a few giant palm trees. Andrew had heard back from the principal, and the new wrestling coach was authorized, so the boys talked about that for a while. Once that topic had been thoroughly covered, Jerry asked Amy about Oklahoma and how she was liking Florida. Amy told him a little about where she used to live and said that she liked the weather in Florida better. It was about that time that the boys finished dinner and grabbed a football.

"So, Gabe tells me you are having some difficulty with your land," Jerry said after the boys were out in the yard playing football.

Amy blushed a little as she answered, "Oh, well, yes, a little. I think I'm making some headway though. It's just hard to get a bank to…" Amy stopped herself.

"To lend money on swampland?" Jerry finished her thought.

"Yes," Amy said bashfully. "I know it seems ridiculous that I bought land that is underwater, but I bought it sight-unseen, and the description didn't mention it was a swamp. Anyway, I guess a lot of the area around me was once underwater."

Jerry nodded without saying a word, and Amy went on, "I've done lots of research, and I know that the land will be great once it is drained. I just have to get the bank to see that. I know how to do it and what is flooding the land too. It's just a matter of diverting the water. It's coming from the Keller ditch. I found out through these people who own a citrus grove near me," Amy said and then took a sip of her margarita.

Jerry had not said a word since Amy started talking about her land, but when she mentioned the Keller ditch, he perked up.

"Do you know who owns the Keller ditch?"

"I don't," she answered. "Why do you ask?"

"Your next step should be to find that out," he told her. "And when you do, I would like to know."

"Okay," Amy said curiously, with inflection that made the statement sound like a question. "Can I ask why?"

"I'm just curious is all," Jerry said as he stared into the rust-colored sky. "I really would like to know, though, as an engineer for the state. These things pique my interest, I guess."

"I see," Amy said. "Well, thank you so much for dinner and a great evening. I don't get out to socialize much, so this has been a real treat for me."

"It has for me as well." Jerry smiled, lifting himself from his cushioned seat. "Thanks so much for coming. I know Gabe loves it when you both do."

The two walked in the house together, where the boys had disappeared to play video games. Amy called back to tell Andy good-bye; he was staying the night with Gabe.

"See you tomorrow, kiddo," Amy said.

"Yup!" Andrew called back, not taking his eyes away from the video game.

"Thanks again, Jerry," Amy said as she stood at the front door.

"The pleasure was mine," Jerry assured her. "And good luck with your land, by the way."

"I'll need it." Amy smiled tiredly, and she headed back for the swamp.

11

As Amy drove home in the quiet darkness of the late evening, an idea sprang into her mind from nowhere. *What if there was some kind of government grant to help with the water removal?* In all her research, she had never thought to look into such a possibility. She had successfully found a way to get rid of the water now, but not a way to pay for the procedure. *What if,* she thought, *the government could help out to get more usable land that could produce revenue for the state?*

As she sailed along the fairly empty, paved road that led past the groves out to her trailer, she felt her mouth go dry and her blood surge through her veins at the thought that there might be a way to get some financial help so she could get her land on the market. As she considered this avenue, it also occurred to her that she had just had dinner with a government engineer. Who else better to ask about government funding on land projects than Jerry?

That thought hung around for days like the smell of smoke and ash after a house fire. The more she thought about it, the more she saw how much Jerry might be able to help. The Swansons had mentioned how they enlisted the help of an engineer to get the water off their land and suggested that she do the same. Amy couldn't help but find the fact that her son had befriended an engineer's son as quite serendipitous, if not lucky, considering her predicament.

Surely, she thought, *he would know if there was anything out there to help me drain this water.* She couldn't stop wondering if there was anything Jerry could do, or any direction Jerry could point her in, to help get rid of the water that kept her from making any money on her property. Her biggest dilemma in finding out was that she wasn't sure if it was appropriate to simply come out and ask him. She thought a lot of both Jerry and Gabe and hated to jeopardize the friendships that were budding by bringing business into the mix. She also feared that it would look like she was using Jerry, which she certainly was not. She vacillated for days and days on what to do.

It's not like I'm asking for free work, she'd tell herself. *I could just make a simple inquiry about whether or not there might be grant money he was aware of, as an engineer, that could help.*

No, she'd tell herself as soon as the first thought floated away. *He'll think I'm trying to get an inside track or hint at something, like borrowing money or getting a favor.*

But you aren't asking him for a favor! She finally decided. *You are simply asking him a question, no more, no less.*

She worked through her tangle of reservations: Would she come off as pushy? Would she seem rude? Was she overstepping her bounds as a new friend? Would Jerry be put out, or even offended, by the inquiry? After she had considered every possible pro and con to asking, she came to the conclusion that it couldn't hurt to ask. So she picked up the phone and dialed Jerry's number.

"Hello?" Jerry said into the receiver.

"Jerry?" Amy asked, holding her breath for a brief moment as she waited for a response.

"This is he."

"Hi, this is Amy…Glade…Andy's mom," she stumbled over her words. It felt as if she were in high school asking the quarterback out to prom.

"Sure, Amy! How are you? Is everything okay?"

"It is," she said, trying to keep her voice steady. "I was just calling…Well, I was wondering if you wanted…if you could meet me for coffee maybe tomorrow or whenever you are free…to talk about my land," she blurted at the end, realizing Jerry may have misconstrued the invite as a date request.

"Sure thing," he said, and she could hear the smile in his voice. Amy felt her nerves unwind a bit as she heard a cheerful and willing response.

"Oh, well, great," she said with an exhale. "How about ten at the Dancing Bean?"

"I'll be there," Jerry said.

The next morning, Amy was up by six, going over what she would say over and over. Andy had stayed the night with Gabe the night before, so she paced the RV and recited out loud the entire conversation. When half past nine rolled around, she had an entire speech worked out.

Jerry was already there when Amy pulled up. He was sitting out on the patio in the sun with two cups of coffee in front of him. Amy felt her heart flutter in her chest when she saw him wave at her. She smiled awkwardly and joined him.

"So did you find out about the owner of the ditch?" he said as he scooted a coffee toward Amy.

"Oh, thank you," Amy said, picking up the coffee and taking a sip. The liquid scalded the tip of her tongue that she choked a little at the surprise of it.

"I haven't yet, actually," she said after she had recovered from the molten hot coffee. "But I have a question in the meantime."

"Shoot," Jerry said.

"Do you know if there might be any funds available for something like what I want to do? I mean, if there might be some government grant or something to remove water to make land usable? I only ask because I have realized how expensive it is, and it seemed like maybe that might be a resource that could help. Since you worked for the army, I just thought you might know about these things. I hate to ask, but…"

"Hmm," Jerry said, sipping his coffee. "I tell ya what. I'll check into it and see if there is money available and how you might get it if there is."

"You have no idea how much I appreciate this." Amy blushed.

"It's no big deal, really," Jerry assured her. "And I would love to help in any way I possibly can. I mean that." He smiled and added, "And don't forget to let me know about that ditch."

"Absolutely," Amy said, her eyes glassy and about to brim over with tears of gratitude. "I will, I promise."

12

Football season came and went, and although the team wasn't great and did not make it to the semifinals, Andrew felt as if he had won the championship. Becoming a part of the team alone, and the friendship that had blossomed between him and Gabe, made the football season a successful one in Andy's eyes, no matter what their record was.

Almost immediately after their last game, it was time to turn their attention to wrestling. Andy was number one on the team and, with all of Andy's extra help, Gabe was number two. The zeal the two had shown for football carried over into wrestling. Amy was there for every match, just like she had been there for every football game; so was Jerry.

Amy saw Jerry a lot over the next couple of months, between the wrestling matches and having Gabe over or Andy going over to the Mulroy's. It started to concern her that Jerry never even mentioned the property or the grant she had asked him about in late September. When November came and he had still skirted the topic every time they saw one another, she started to lose hope. She took on the attitude that no news was bad news, and so it was back to the drawing board for her.

Night after night, Amy poured over the initial research she had done about the various ways to drain land. She looked over the costs of each and the time they took. Even the cheapest way to get rid of the water was far too much for her, especially since she was paying for Andrew's car now. Everything took money—money that Amy did not have.

One evening, while Amy was going over the budget and trying to find ways to cut costs any way she could to put more back into savings, her phone started to buzz away on the table. It was her cousin Joy from Kansas. *How strange*, she thought as she picked up her phone, she had not talked to Joy for some time, but the two had been very close throughout childhood. So close, in fact, that she always viewed Joy's mother, Loraine, as her own mother. She suddenly felt a twinge that she hadn't seen them in such a long time.

"Hi there, stranger," Amy said into her phone.

"Hello, Amy?" Joy said, and her voice was nasally and muffled.

"Joy? Is everything okay?"

"Mama's passed, Amy," Joy bawled. "She's gone."

"Oh, Joy," Amy said falling back into the bench seat of the kitchenette. "I am so sorry, Joy. I just can't…I should have been there with you."

"Well, you know she had dementia, so she wouldn't have known either way," Joy said.

"But I should've been there for you. I am so sorry, Joy. I can be there in no time to help with arrangements and all. Let me at least do that. You know I loved Auntie L like she was my own mom," Amy said, feeling intense sadness bubble up at the back of her throat.

"Mama had everything all planned out and paid for, hon, so don't worry about that. And she knew you loved her. We all know it's been hard with that son of a gun you were married to, so don't you worry."

"That's no excuse. I just feel so awful," Amy said, starting to sob.

"Well, I have something to tell you that I hope brightens your day, sweetie" Joy said, her voice clearing and the sadness falling from her words. "It turns out that Mama had accumulated quite a bit of wealth that none of us knew about from mineral rights she got from my great-granddad. She left you thirty thousand dollars, Amy. Can you believe it?"

Amy's words caught in her throat, and she nearly dropped her phone. "What?" she finally forced out.

"Yup, she left everyone a good chunk since she only had two kids, two nieces, and one nephew total. You all each got the thirty thousand. I know it ain't appropriate to say, but she left me and James three hundred thousand dollars apiece. Can you even believe that? She was so sly, Mama was."

"I just don't even know how to react right now," Amy sputtered. "I mean, I really don't. Auntie L was always an angel. I can't even believe she did this. I feel like I don't even deserve it."

"Well, Mama sure thought you did, and you know how she hated people arguing with her," Joy said with a chuckle. "We'll get you the check within the week. And Mama asked that there be no funeral. Said she wants people to go out and have fun and think of her, not sit up in a church bawlin' their eyes out. If you guys ever want to visit her grave though, she's gonna be buried at the family cemetery up near Selena. She was pretty adamant about not making a fuss too, so you just enjoy that money."

"Thank you so much, Joy," Amy spewed. "I mean, you have no idea. You just have no idea what a godsend this is."

"I'm glad to hear it. You take care and don't be a stranger."

Amy rushed into town to find Andrew to tell him the news. He had stayed in town to go eat with Gabe, and Amy could not wait for him to get home. When she spotted his car at the little burger-and-shake shack, she pulled in and hardly had the car in park before she jumped out of it.

"Mom?" Andrew said as he chewed a wad of burger and fries. "What's going on?"

"You are not going to believe this, Andy," she panted.

"What?"

"Auntie L has passed."

"That's awful," Andy said.

"I know, it is. But she left us…" Amy looked around and realized she was talking so that the whole place could hear her, so she leaned in and whispered. "She left us thirty thousand dollars, Andy! Can you believe that?" she said in an excited whisper.

"Shut up!"

"I'm serious. Now you guys get rid of those burgers because we are going somewhere nice!" Amy announced.

Amy knew that the money wasn't enough to drain the land yet, but she took solace in the fact that for the first time, she would be debt-free and have a little cash on hand. She could pay off Andrew's car and all her expenses, at least, so that all her income could go toward saving for the water removal. It may have not paid for it directly, but she felt in her heart it was going to help get her there one way or another; she just had to figure out how.

13

Just one week after Amy received the call from Joy, she got a call from someone else that brought her even more good news. It was Jerry. After two months of no word, he finally called to talk about something other than the boys or meeting up to go grab a bite to eat or see a movie, as the two had begun spending time, just the two of them, when the boys were out messing around town. Both told themselves it was all platonic.

"I think I have some good news for you, Amy," he said.

"Go on."

"I know I haven't said anything about it in a while, but that is because I didn't want to get your hopes up."

"Okay," Amy said, about to explode with curiosity.

"So I've been talking to the higher-ups about your place. They started doing some research of their own about it and they want to finance the water diversion. How about that!"

"Say again," Amy gasped.

"We're going to divert the water from the Keller ditch to another location to dry out your land, Amy! And the government is picking up the tab!"

"This can't be real," Amy mumbled. "I mean, this has got to be a dream. Tell me this is real, Jerry."

"Oh, it is. Now there will be some stipulations. You will be responsible for pumping the water out of the property. Also, once the land starts making money, you will have to pay a percentage to the government for a time, but it's nothing compared to what you'll make."

"But why?" Amy asked. "I mean, I hate to look a gift horse in the mouth, but this sounds too good to be true."

"Well, one is because we need more usable land. I gave them your research to show how well the other pieces of property have done after being drained and showed what kind of income it could bring to the state, so it is a good investment, especially if you pay back a percentage on profit for a set amount of time."

"So I just have to pay a percentage and pump the water off?"

"Looks like it."

"I actually have any idea of what to do with the water that I pump off."

"That's good news. You're ahead of the eight ball then. What were you thinking?"

"When I was traveling around the area doing research, I saw a few places that were actually buying water, for orange groves mostly. There are groves everywhere around here. Surely one of them could use it."

"That sounds like a plan!" Jerry said. "Oh, and by the way, the ditch is owned by a company that works with the government quite a bit. That's the other reason my supervisors said yes. That's why I wondered about it in the first place, just FYI. I just didn't want to say and get your hopes up."

"I totally forgot about that." Amy sighed. "Thanks so much, Jerry. You are an angel. I mean it."

The next day, Amy went around to the nearby groves asking if any of them could use the water she'd be pumping off her land. As it turned out, a couple of groves did indeed need water, so much so that one of the owners was willing to pay for both the pump and pipeline to get the water to their land so long as Amy would sign a contract promising that she would continue to provide them with water, and no one else.

"Thank you so much," Amy said as she got up to leave.

"They say the next war will be fought over water, not oil or gold," the man said as he shook Amy's hand. "I like the idea that I'll be getting it pumped onto my farm. Helps me sleep at night knowing my crop won't dry up and wither away."

The next weeks were full of legal transactions, the signing of contracts and documents between Amy and the US government and Amy and the grove owner, and a lot of blood, sweat, and tears. Amy stopped in the middle of it all to look around her one day. In the midst of her utter happiness, she felt a pessimism lurking beneath—a feeling in the pit of her stomach that nagged her and hinted that all this was just too good to be true. She shoved the bad feeling deep down inside her and continued on. She fought hard for this; she earned it. There was nothing, as far as she could tell, that could stop her now.

Everything seemed to fall right into place. Once the trenches had been dug, the pipes and pumps installed, and the water drained, Amy started to work with developers. The Army Corp engineers were able to verify that the land was perfect for any purpose, and so the bank finally gave Amy her loan for development.

"I think you should call it Amy Ranch." Andrew smiled. "You fought hard for this. I think you deserve some credit."

"I don't know," Amy replied. "Would it be silly to name it after me?"

"Shoot, I would!" Gabe chimed in.

"Amy Ranch it is then!" she said excitedly.

With the name decided, it was time for the fun part. Amy worked closely with all the contractors every step of the way, with Jerry's help. She decided that the development would consist of large-building custom lots and it would have an impressive Arnold Palmer-designed golf course in the middle of it all. She scrutinized over every detail, from the placement of the lots to the type of landscaping they'd use. She and Jerry even worked closely with the civil engineers and land surveyors to design the streets just so.

Amy's hard work paid off. The project was an immediate financial success. Once the lots were put on the market, most were gone before Amy could even blink. It was the most exciting time of her life. Other than the birth of Andrew, it was also the most amazing thing she had ever experienced. But a rain cloud settled heavy over her little celebration when a familiar Ford Ranger pickup pulled up one day to the main office that doubled as Amy and Andrew's home.

It was Dale, and he was accompanied by a younger woman with wild, bleach-blond hair so dry and frazzled that it looked like it could fall right out of her head at any moment. The young woman wore a shirt that stopped just above her pierced belly button and had a barbed wire tattoo that circled her left, overly-tanned bicep. Amy noticed that they both wore wedding bands; hers was huge and unsightly. Amy felt a little petty when she scoffed looking at it and immediately thought to herself how it must be a fake. Her eyes were soon diverted from the chunk of cubic zirconium on the woman's finger to Dale. She could see just in the way he got out of his truck that he was not there to wish her well. She was right about that.

14

Dale barged into the entry of the office/model home with a ferocity that Amy had come to know very well, and was very happy to be rid of the last several months. Amy stood up from behind her large oak desk and braced herself for whatever it was Dale was about to do.

"Can I help you, Dale?" she said coldly.

"Yeah, you can help me," he spat. "You can help me by giving me what's mine."

"I don't know what that means, Dale." Amy sighed.

"Oh, you don't?" Dale asked mockingly, his new wife hanging on his arm, giving Amy a searing glare.

"No, I don't. We signed divorce papers months ago. We agreed on everything then. You got everything you said you wanted."

"I want my percentage of all this," he said, waving his arms around wildly as if he were swatting invisible mosquitoes. "This is at least half mine—at least," he shouted.

"You signed the papers that gave up the land, Dale," Amy reminded him.

"Yeah, well I came to contest all that."

"On what grounds?" Amy demanded.

"On the grounds that I was not represented properly," he fumed. "I owned half of the property and I deserve half of the profits. I've already started the paperwork, Miss Hot Shot. You'll be receiving notice from my lawyer soon," he snorted then turned and left, his new wife trailing behind him like cheap perfume.

"You don't want to ask about your son then, I guess?" Amy called after him. She took a step backwards after she had said this, surprised that the words had escaped her.

"Excuse me?" Dale stopped and pivoted around to face Amy again. He stopped so abruptly that his wife slammed into him and nearly fell back on her behind.

"All you have to say is 'Where's my money?'" Amy said, standing her ground. "When's the last time you talked to Andrew?"

"Phone works both ways," he snapped. "That boy's a mama's boy and a trader anyway."

"Very mature, especially coming from *you*," Amy retorted.

"You just get yourself ready, Amy. Because I'll get what's mine."

Dale left Amy shaking behind her desk. She was so riled up by his sudden appearance. She couldn't believe the nerve he had. She hadn't heard a word or received a cent in child support since the divorce, and out of nowhere he showed up yelling about what was his. She wondered how he even found out about the land in the first place since he hardly called to talk to his son. It was just like Dale to vanish until he thought showing up would help him out.

Within twenty-four hours, Amy received a notice of contention from a tall, sinewy man with a receding hairline and heavy glasses. As she read over the notice, her blood boiled. She realized she had done everything on her own. Dale had done nothing but tell her she was a failure since they showed up to Florida—better, since they had met—and now he was trying to swoop in and take what she had earned. Amy may have cowered to him in the past, but she would not cower anymore; she would fight back. With all her might, she would take Dale on and win.

Amy knew that first and foremost, she needed a lawyer, but she didn't know a single lawyer in the state of Florida, so she went to Jerry to ask for his advice about what to do and who to go to since he was familiar with both land law and the local attorneys. He suggested that she consult with the best real estate attorney in the area, a man named Aris Doyle.

"I've seen him win more land dispute cases than I can count," Jerry said. "He's a straight shooter and the best at what he does."

The next day, she called Doyle's office in Miami. She explained her predicament over the phone. After she was done, Doyle told her, "I'd be happy to take the case, but I will tell you that it is going to be expensive."

"That is fine," Amy said. "As long as my ex doesn't steal what isn't his."

"I assure you, he won't," Doyle said confidently.

The trail would take place in two months in Fort Lauderdale, Florida. Those two months, Amy spent all her free time with Doyle, working up their plan of attack. Jerry accompanied her to many of their meetings, mostly for support. Doyle prepared her in every way possible and was sure to let her know that these kinds of hearings were generally very emotionally taxing.

"If this Dale is a real bastard, then he'll do all he can to make you out to be a crook," he told her. "I mean, imagine him on his worst day and multiply it by ten."

"I don't know if he could get any worse than he has been," Amy said.

"He can and he will," Doyle told her. "So get ready for it. And tell your son the same. These kinds of guys, nothing is off limits to them."

"You could say that again," Amy mumbled.

The trial finally arrived after weeks of preparation. Doyle was correct about Dale; he was more venomous than he had ever been, and he was not afraid to lie on the stand if he had to. They spent days in the courtroom, going over documents and battling it out.

"She just waited to get me out there and divorce me so she could use all my money and then kick me to the curb!" Dale said at one point. "She knew just what she was doing the whole time. And now she has turned my son against me and bled me dry."

Amy could hardly believe her ears. Dale was rotten, she knew, but she was surprised at how rotten he really was. She tried to keep from showing any emotion during the process, no matter how difficult it was. She refused to let Dale get the best of her.

The trial came down to one key witness—the one person who had been there to see it all happen, Andrew. Amy wanted to keep Andrew out of the hot seat, and she fought to do so, but at the end of the trial, they had no choice. Andrew would have to testify in court. Amy could barely stand to watch, but she was baffled when Andrew took the stand. He was calm and confident, unshaken by it all.

"My mother has worked her tail off since we got here," he said, sitting in the small witness stand. "She has not stopped working, paying the bills, and taking care of me since my dad left us. She has been the most selfless person I ever met through this. I could see she was losing hope there at the end,"

Andrew said, glancing over at Amy. "She had tried everything she could, but nothing was working. She didn't know it, but I used to stay awake and listen to her cry after she thought I was asleep as she looked over the mountains of research she had. But then finally, things worked out. She got a little money from her aunt who died, and then my best friend's dad was able to help. I don't think anyone else would've made it, but my mom, she's a fighter. She taught me how to fight back, and that's what she did. And she made it work. Everyone said she couldn't do it, but she fought and she succeeded. My dad, he thought she'd fail. He said so before he left us. But Mom didn't give up. She fought back," Andy said, glaring a hole through Dale.

The day after Andrew took the stand, the judge made his final decision. Andrew and Amy stood hand in hand in the courtroom, holding their breath. Dale stood glaring at the two of them. When the judge finally read his ruling, the two collapsed on each other. Amy had won the case. Dale would get nothing since he had already signed away the land to Amy, fair and square. They had won.

15

Amy and Andrew returned to Middletown smiling ear to ear. The next week, Andrew wrestled in his last tournament; it was for the state championship. With the help of Coach Jennings, the team had gone almost undefeated; Andrew himself had a perfect record. As always, Amy and Jerry sat side by side and watched their boys wrestle their last matches. When the tournament ended, Middletown had taken the title by a landslide. As Gabe and Andrew celebrated on the mat, up in the stands Jerry and Amy wrapped their arms around one another. It was then that Jerry leaned back and did something that caught Amy completely off guard. He leaned down and kissed her in the middle of all the excitement. As his lips met hers, she was first shocked, and she nearly pulled away, but then she relaxed and melted into the kiss. She felt her blood buzz through her body and realized she had never felt a kiss quite like that.

"I guess it's not platonic after all," Jerry said slyly as the two took a step back and looked at one another.

"I guess not." Amy smiled and slipped her hand in his.

As Gabe and Andrew started for their parents after the tournament, they were stopped by a husky man with a blue sports coat and oiled hair. His name was Tim Johnson, he told the two boys, and he was a scout from Florida State.

"I'm glad you two are together, actually," the stout man said as he tapped the red plastic clipboard he was holding, "because I wanted to talk to you both about coming on at Florida State next year. It looks like you boys could get yourself a scholarship, wrestling like that."

Amy and Jerry walked up as the scout talked to the boys and handed them each an envelope with some information.

"What's going on over here?" Jerry asked cheerfully.

"Florida State is offering us a scholarship!" Gabe blurted. "Both of us!"

"Is that true?" Amy asked, bringing her small hand to her chest in surprise.

"Yes, ma'am, it is. I'd love to have these boys on our team. They have all the info right in those packets," Johnson said, pointing a thick finger at the envelope Gabe was holding. "Just take a look at it and get back to us ASAP," he said, holding his giant paw out to Amy.

Amy shook Tim's hand and then Jerry did the same. After the sturdy scout lumbered off, Amy wrapped her arms around Andrew and kissed his sweaty, raw cheek.

"I am so proud of you, Andy!" she beamed. "You don't even know how proud I am."

"I'm proud of you too, Mom," he told her.

"It's been a big year for all of us, hasn't it?" Amy said, looking at the group.

"The best of my life," Andrew said.

"Mine too," Jerry grinned, looking at Amy. "Speaking of this big year, once you boys get changed, we're all going out somewhere nice to celebrate. We also have something to tell you."

"What?" Gabe asked.

"Just get changed. You'll see," Jerry insisted.

"What do you think it is?" Andrew asked as he and Gabe made their way to the locker room.

"I have no idea," Gabe said. "But I imagine it's good. Did you see the way my dad said that? He looked like he was half-drunk the way he talked. His eyes even looked glassy!"

"I can't imagine what could be better than the news we just heard from that scout."

"Maybe our parents are hooking up." Gabe grinned slyly, jabbing Andrew in the ribs with his elbow.

"Right," Andrew scoffed. "I think that ship has sailed, man."

That night at dinner, Amy and Jerry told the boys their big news. Gabe clapped his hands in pleasure and shouted,

"I knew it!" Amy scooted closer to Jerry and put her arm around him.

"How do you feel about it, Andy?" she asked her son, who hadn't said much.

"I just...I just can't believe how awesome my life is right now." He smiled.

"Neither can I, bud. But I guess we'd better get used to it." She grinned.

That night after dinner, Amy went back to Jerry's and they talked for hours about what came next. They decided that marriage seemed the best next step, but they'd have at least a year-long engagement to plan everything and let the boys get used to it. They didn't finish talking until after midnight

"I better get home," Amy yawned as she glanced at the clock behind her on the wall.

"Just stay," Jerry suggested.

"Not until we say 'I do,'" Amy teased. "We want to set a good example, right?"

"We'll see." Jerry grinned tiredly. "Are you sure you're okay to drive?"

"Absolutely," she said. "I'm still going on adrenaline."

"Call me when you get there so I won't worry?"

"Will do," she said.

Driving back under the starry Florida sky, Amy reflected on everything that had happened the last year of her life. She thought about how far Andrew had come from the boy who had been picked on by all the bullies back in Oklahoma. She realized at that moment that the lesson she had taught him about fighting back was the greatest thing she could have done for her son. Then all of a sudden, she realized that she had been doing the same thing with her own life. Andrew was going to go to college on a wrestling scholarship, and she was the founder of Amy Ranch, and it all started when they learned how to fight back. She had no idea when she first taught her son a life lesson about standing up for himself that she would end up learning a much greater lesson from him. She smiled at how strange and wonderful life can be.

AUTHOR'S OTHER WORKS

This book is one of the five books written by Dr. Melvin J. Bagley in the last five years. His first book is Son of a Gun, a cowboy story about a young kid who is fast with a gun and ends up in a shootout with a gunslinger while protecting his mother.

Dr. Bagley's second book is Old Bones, a murder mystery about a schoolteacher who takes one year out of teaching to go back to school in an attempt to crack a case that the Michigan State Police cannot solve.

The third book is Celerity Sighting, a collection of letters accompanying the many pairs of glasses sent to Dr. Melvin

J. Bagley that are to be displayed in The Famous People's Eyeglasses Museum.

The fourth book is Fight Back, a story about a mother who teaches her young son who is being bullied in school to fight back. By the end of the tale, the young son teaches his mother the same lesson when he shows her that she too has been bullied by her husband.

The fifth book is Giggs, a story about a guy who takes five unpopular girls to prom and changes their lives in amazing ways. The protagonist becomes fabulously rich but does it all on borrowed money, eventually losing everything.

Any of these books can be purchased at Amazon.com or any bookstore. Any profits to be derived from any of the sale of the books will be donated to the Primary Children Hospital in Salt Lake City, Utah.